"What...
are these?"

King's Proposal
The Witch of Resplendent Color

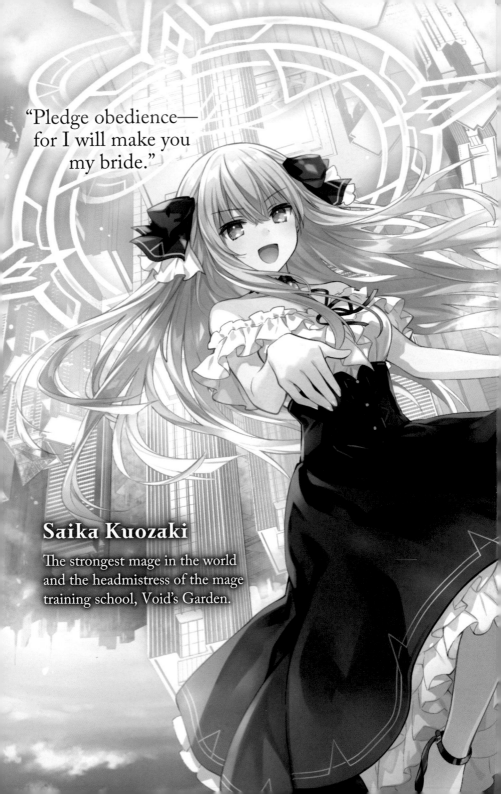

"Pledge obedience—
for I will make you
my bride."

Saika Kuozaki

The strongest mage in the world
and the headmistress of the mage
training school, Void's Garden.

"I guess there's no need to hold back, huh...?!"

"Silence! Fight on your own time!"

"Starting tomorrow, Lady Saika will be attending the Garden as a student."

Anviet Svarner
A Knight of the Garden. A bellicose instructor.

Kuroe Karasuma
Saika's attendant. The only person at the Garden aware of Saika's death.

Erulka Flaera
A Knight of the Garden. Responsible for the Garden's medical department and the second oldest mage after Saika.

"...There are times when a woman has to fight, even when she knows she shouldn't...!"

"Nice to meet you, everyone."

Ruri Fuyajoh

A Knight of the Garden under Saika's direct command. A student with an obsessive adoration for Saika and her brother Mushiki.

"Be quiet. Your hands are flailing about—no, maybe your mouth?"

"Um, Kuroe...?
What are you...?"

Mushiki Kuga

A young man who inherits
Saika's body and powers.

"I'm glad it was you who found me."

CONTENTS

KING'S PROPOSAL

Volume 1

The Witch of
❖ Resplendent Color ❖

Koushi Tachibana

Illustration by **Tsunako**

YEN
ON

NEW YORK

KING'S PROPOSAL

Vol. 1

Koushi Tachibana

Translation by Haydn Trowell
Cover art by Tsunako

OSAMA NO PROPOSAL Vol. 1 GOKUSAI NO MAJO
©Koushi Tachibana, Tsunako 2021
First published in Japan in 2021 by KADOKAWA CORPORATION, Tokyo.
English translation rights arranged with KADOKAWA CORPORATION, Tokyo, through TUTTLE-MORI AGENCY, INC., Tokyo.

English translation © 2022 by Yen Press, LLC

Yen On
150 West 30th Street, 19th Floor
New York, NY 10001

Visit us at yenpress.com
facebook.com/yenpress
twitter.com/yenpress
yenpress.tumblr.com
instagram.com/yenpress

First Yen On Edition: November 2022
Edited by Yen On Editorial: Shella Wu, Payton Campbell
Designed by Yen Press Design: Madelaine Norman, Wendy Chan

Yen On is an imprint of Yen Press, LLC.
The Yen On name and logo are trademarks of Yen Press, LLC.

Library of Congress Cataloging-in-Publication Data
Names: Tachibana, Koushi, 1986- author. | Tsunako, illustrator. | Trowell, Haydn, translator.
Title: King's proposal / Koushi Tachibana ; illustration by Tsunako ; translation by Haydn Trowell.
Other titles: Osama no proposal. English
Description: First Yen On edition. | New York, NY : Yen On, 2022- |
Contents: v. 1. The Witch of Resplendent Color
Identifiers: LCCN 2022027184 | ISBN 9781975351502 (v. 1 ; trade paperback)
Subjects: CYAC: Fantasy. | Witches—Fiction. | Magic—Fiction. | Schools—Fiction. | Identity—Fiction. | LCGFT: Fantasy fiction. | Witch fiction. | School fiction. | Light novels.
Classification: LCC PZ7.1.T296 Kin 2022 | DDC [Fic]—dc23
LC record available at https://lccn.loc.gov/2022027184

ISBNs: 978-1-9753-5150-2 (paperback)
          978-1-9753-5151-9 (ebook)

10 9 8 7 6 5 4 3 2 1

LSC-C

Printed in the United States of America

KING'S PROPOSAL

The Witch of Resplendent Color

In sickness and in health.

For better and for worse.

For richer and for poorer.

Not parted even in death.

I entrust you with my world.

Prologue
⊷ First Love ⊷

Mushiki Kuga's first love was a corpse.

"..."

He stood there, his heart throbbing, a deep sigh escaping his lips, unable to comprehend the maelstrom of emotions swirling within his chest.

Mushiki was neither a grotesque murderer nor a necromaniac.

At the very least, he had never killed anyone before, nor had he ever collected pictures of dead bodies. If anything, he was just as averse to such sights as anyone else.

But now he found himself unable to look away from the scene in front of him.

The girl was lying on her back, covered in blood.

She must have been around sixteen or seventeen years old.

Her face still showed traces of a lingering innocence and gave a glimpse of a certain allure on the verge of coming into flower.

In the glow of the streetlights, her long hair shimmered in a hue that wasn't gold or silver.

Her eyes were tightly closed, so Mushiki couldn't discern the color of her irises, but her expression only served to reinforce her well-defined

nose and lips, emphasizing her somewhat inhuman beauty—almost as though he was staring at a porcelain doll.

Finally, as if to apply color to that beguiling figure, blood was smeared on her chest like a bright-red rose, even now still slowly expanding across the fabric of her dress.

It was horrible. Cruel. Brutal.

But most of all, it was dizzyingly beautiful.

Ah yes. There could be no doubt about it.

For the first time in his life, Mushiki felt something he had never experienced before.

He had fallen in love with this girl.

"...Y-you..."

"...!"

After a long, drawn-out pause, a weak and ephemeral voice, almost extinguished, brought him back to his senses.

It was the girl, lying fallen on the ground, who had called out to him with labored breath.

She was still alive.

Mushiki suddenly felt ashamed at having jumped to the wrong conclusion.

Though, more importantly, he was relieved to see she was still conscious.

"Are you okay?! What happened to you?!" he cried out in a tremulous voice as he knelt by her side.

He still didn't know what was going on, and his thoughts were an absolute mess.

All the same, due to his sense of duty to save her, he managed to maintain his composure, albeit just barely.

The girl's eyes fluttered open.

A pair of fantastical eyes, alight in every color imaginable, slowly studied his face.

"...H-hah... I—I see... So this...this is... Ah... I'm glad...it was you... here at the end..."

"What...?"

Mushiki failed to understand the meaning behind the girl's words, and confusion was plain on his face.

Maybe the loss of blood was making her delirious. That wouldn't be at all unsurprising. She needed medical attention as soon as possible.

However, there was no such equipment nearby, and even if there had been, he wouldn't have known how to treat her. He tried calling an ambulance, but his phone seemed to be out of range.

As such, his only option was to carry her to a hospital himself.

But where on earth was he to go, what with the world having *changed* so profoundly?

"—!"

At that moment, Mushiki looked up at the sound of footsteps echoing behind him.

There was no telling the identity of the approaching figure, but regardless, this was a godsend. Mushiki wasn't skilled enough to save the girl by himself. He stood and began to turn around to ask for help, when—

"...D-don't. Run—"

"...Ugh..."

The girl didn't even have time to finish her sentence.

Mushiki let out a stunned gasp as a fiery pain tore through his chest.

He looked down, only to see a red blossom of blood almost identical to the girl's own wound unfurling its petals across his torso.

Only then did he comprehend.

Whoever had appeared behind him had just impaled him through the chest.

"Ugh... Ah..."

By the time he had fully processed what had happened, his body was no longer responding to his thoughts.

His vision was going dark, and the strength left his limbs.

The pain was so intense that he could hardly breathe.

Unable to remain standing, he collapsed to the ground by the girl's side.

"…"

The footsteps fading into the distance told him that their attacker was slowly departing.

Mushiki was in no state to pursue—or even to confirm the identity of their assailant.

As he heaved a cough, blood spewed from his throat, trickling down his cheek to the ground.

His awareness, overcome by agonizing pain, was gradually fading.

His sense of touch weakening, that of taste disappearing, of smell dulling, while his vision slowly blurred.

In the midst of those vague sensations, there *was* something that broke through, faint though it was.

The girl by his side crawled over to him with her last ounces of strength and fell sprawled over his limp body.

"…I'm sorry. I didn't mean…to drag you into this… But it can't be helped now. I'm going to have to stick with you…until the end…"

The girl placed her hand on Mushiki's cheek—and pressed her lips against his.

"…"

Their blood mixed together.

A first kiss that left a horrid aftertaste—the metallic tang of blood.

Nonetheless, Mushiki, his senses leaving him, was unable to respond.

He was already on the verge of blacking out.

With his last remaining strength, he heard the girl whisper something close to his ear.

"…I'm entrusting you with my world…"

Chapter 1
⊰ Coalescence ⊱

"Ngh... Ugh..."

Mushiki awoke to find himself lying in a luxurious canopied bed.

After blinking a few times, he cast his gaze around the room.

It was large, the walls covered with antique shelves and closets. Beside his pillow was a stylish little lamp. A plush carpet covered the floor, shining magnificently with the light glimmering in through the gaps between the drawn curtains.

It was a dazzling awakening in this beautiful bedroom, and the elegance of it all was rather striking.

The only problem was that it was all utterly foreign to him.

"What the...?"

A murmur escaped his lips. Maybe it was because he had just woken up, but his ears were ringing, and he could hardly make out his own voice.

Baffled, he tried to recall his memories to figure out what might have brought him here.

His name was Mushiki Kuga. He was seventeen years old, a high school student, and lived in the city of Ohjoh in Tokyo. He remembered that much.

His last memory before falling asleep...had him walking the familiar road home.

Right. He had been on his way back from school. Clearly, *something* must have happened for him to be waking up here.

...Had he been abducted? Was he the victim of a hit-and-run, sending him off to heaven? Or had he spent the night with a woman who had gotten horribly drunk somewhere...? But none of those possibilities seemed particularly likely.

All that being the case, then maybe he was still dreaming?

His senses still dull, he tried pinching his cheek. It didn't hurt all that much, but he couldn't tell if that was because he really was dreaming or if his fingers were simply sapped of strength.

In any case, there was no point staying in bed.

Stepping down onto the floor, he slid his feet into the slippers laid out for him, crossed the room unsteadily, and opened the door, when—

"...Huh?"

His eyes widened in shock.

As soon as he walked through the doorway, it was as though he had been instantly transported to some unknown destination. The scenery was completely unknown to him.

The sun lit up the deep-blue sky, and a straight paved road stretched along the ground outside, with fountains and trees dotting its length as though to punctuate it with nature. At the end of the thoroughfare, a magnificent building towered above it all like a king perched atop his throne.

This sight was completely at odds with his everyday life, and yet something about it reminded him of the buildings and facilities at school.

Glancing over his shoulder, he was even more taken aback.

There was no sign of the bedroom where he had been until just a moment ago.

Unable to grasp what was going on, he rested a shaky hand on his forehead.

"...I guess I *am* still dreaming?"

Nonetheless, it looked like he wouldn't have time to continue fretting over this situation.

The reason for that was simple. Unlike the room he had just stepped out of, there were people here walking to and fro.

Maybe they were students? Boys and girls in matching uniforms were proceeding in groups toward the huge building up ahead.

A few of them, perhaps startled by his sudden appearance, stopped in their tracks, glancing his way wide-eyed.

"Um..."

Who *wouldn't* be surprised to see someone pop up out of thin air like this...? Though, in truth, no one was more taken aback than Mushiki himself.

Anyway, for now, he would have to find a way to explain that he wasn't a suspicious person—and at the same time try to figure out where he was.

He turned to the girl closest to him. "Um..."

Before he could even finish his thought—

"Good morning, Madam Witch!"

The girl gave a reverent curtsy as she called out in greeting.

"...Huh?"

His eyes widened in surprise at this unexpected response.

Before he knew it, the other students standing around him likewise began to offer salutations.

"Morning."

"How are you today, Madam Witch?"

"You look radiant this morning!"

All the while, Mushiki stood there petrified, like a deer in headlights.

"...?"

That wasn't all. The next moment, an older man, probably a teacher, appeared behind him.

"Good morning, Headmistress," the man greeted him politely.

Madam Witch.

Headmistress.

Mushiki could only tilt his head to one side in even greater consternation as person after person continued to address him with those unfamiliar titles.

At the very least, he didn't remember anyone ever having spoken to him like that before.

Moreover, neither title seemed particularly apt for a male high school student like himself.

"...Hmm?"

Confused, he found himself glancing down at his own body—and only then did he finally notice it.

He couldn't see his own feet.

Or strictly speaking, there was something blocking his line of vision.

"What...are these?"

Two large, unfamiliar masses hung from his chest.

Recovering slightly from his shock, Mushiki reached out to touch them with his hands.

"...What?!"

At that moment, his fingers dug into something soft—and he instantly felt a faint, sweet stimulation course through his chest.

"I-it can't be..."

They clearly weren't fake.

Those soft masses were part of his own body.

And now that he stopped to think about it, the fingers and hands exploring them were slenderer and paler in color than he remembered them being.

"..."

Having put two and two together, he took off running, until finally he reached a fountain by the roadside and peered into the water.

Seeing the reflection of the face staring back at him, he was rendered speechless.

That was only natural. What he saw wasn't his own familiar countenance, the face of a high school boy, but rather that of a beautiful woman endowed with long, gorgeous hair and bright, iridescent eyes.

"..."

Yep. There could be no doubt about it.

He had somehow *become* a girl. To put it mildly, it made no sense. Everything had been one inexplicable sight after another since he had woken up, but it all paled in comparison to *this*. It was too preposterous to be a dream.

Though to be fair, Mushiki's speechlessness wasn't only due to the fact that he had somehow been turned into a girl.

No, there was a much simpler, more romantic, more absurd reason for his loss of words.

In short, just like Narcissus in the ancient Greek myth, he had fallen utterly in love with the reflection staring back at him in the water.

Only half aware of his own actions, he reached out to touch her cheek.

He could feel his heart thumping, the sound growing louder and louder.

His brain felt like it was about to be overloaded by the unending stream of information that his eyes were feeding to it.

It was unbelievable, terrifying even—and a wonderfully sweet sensation.

Of course, the girl in the reflection was beautiful to behold. Her almond-shaped eyes. The well-defined bridge of her nose. Her luscious lips. It was no exaggeration to say that her features were perfectly balanced—a miraculous, sublime work of art.

But that wasn't all.

No, that wasn't enough to explain the intensity of emotion welling up inside him.

Ah, *now* he understood, an eerie conviction taking root.

There could be no doubt about it. The word that those wise minds from the past had coined in order to express this inexplicable rush of feelings could be none other than *love*.

"Am I...in love with her...? No, with *myself*...?" he whispered in awe before catching his breath.

His memories flooded back to him as he looked upon that face, almost as if they had been waiting for this opportunity.

Right. He knew this girl.

How could he have forgotten? He had met her just before he had lost consciousness.

She was the girl with the flower-shaped bloodstain on her chest.

"Here you are."

A voice like a small chime ringing came from behind him, prompting Mushiki to raise his face with a start.

"Huh...?"

Looking over his shoulder, he noticed a small girl standing there.

Her short black hair was pulled back tightly in a bun, and her clothes were similar in color. Her eyes, peering into Mushiki's face, were likewise black obsidian.

"...M-me, you mean?" he said, pointing to himself.

Though her expression remained unchanged, the girl had just realized something.

"My apologies. I take it your memories have yet to be fully integrated? You must be rather confused, I take it?" She paused for a moment before continuing: "I'm Kuroe Karasuma, attendant to the person *you have become*. I've been fully briefed on how to proceed should this unlikely development come to pass." With that, she gave him a polite bow.

Mushiki hurried to stand up straight. "...! Do you know something?! Tell me! Just who am I?!"

In response to these questions, the girl, Kuroe, gave him a brief nod. "My lady's name is Saika Kuozaki—the most powerful mage in the world."

"Wha—?"

Mushiki's eyes snapped open at this shocking declaration.

Then, still gripped by the powerful urge that had taken hold of his chest, he murmured:

"What...what a beautiful name..."

"...Excuse me?"

"Huh?"

Kuroe and Mushiki, staring at each other in wonder, both tilted their heads in puzzlement.

◇

Twenty minutes had passed since their encounter by the fountain. Mushiki had followed Kuroe to the huge structure towering over the end of the paved road—the central school building.

They were on the top floor, in a room labeled the HEADMISTRESS'S OFFICE on the sign by the door. It was a large space filled with modern equipment, but combined with the bookshelves packed with old-fashioned tomes alongside ancient-looking tools scattered around the walls, it served to give the room a strangely eclectic look.

Standing in the middle of the room, Mushiki was at pains trying to explain how he had ended up in this situation.

All the while, Kuroe, for some reason, after sitting him down in front of a mirror, was busy carefully combing his hair.

Apparently, she couldn't let him be seen with hair in such disarray after just getting out of bed.

"I see. On your way back from school, you found yourself wandering into a mysterious space, where you stumbled on Lady Saika covered in blood. After that, someone attacked you from behind, you lost consciousness, and then you woke up here. Yes?" Kuroe asked after repeating his story back to him.

"That's right," Mushiki answered.

"When you say a *mysterious space*, what specifically do you mean?"

"Um... Well, how do I put it? There were all these tall buildings lined up in rows, and it was kinda like a maze or a labyrinth...," Mushiki explained, gesturing with his hands.

Kuroe slightly frowned. "A fourth substantiation... So it really was a mage... But who could be capable of forging a space like that...?"

"Huh?"

"No, it's nothing," Kuroe said with a shake of her head before placing the comb back on the table and tying his hair with a frilly ribbon. "Thank you. I believe I now have a solid grasp of the situation."

The beauty staring back at him in the mirror had soared to yet greater heights. Utterly captivated, Mushiki sighed.

"She's incredible... It's like it isn't really me..."

"Strictly speaking, that's exactly right."

"Ah, I guess it is..."

Mushiki spun around on his chair to get a better look at the other girl.

"So, um... Ms. Kuroe?"

"Just Kuroe will do. I'm afraid it feels rather unnatural to be addressed so politely by that face."

"..." Though slightly uneasy about the master-servant relationship that he had found himself in, Mushiki decided to play along. "Um, Kuroe, then. There are some things I want to ask you, too..."

"I'm sure there are. It's quite expected for you to be confused right now. Please, ask me anything. If I can answer your questions, I will," she said with a nod.

Mushiki took her up on that offer. "So this girl... You said her name is Saika, right?"

"Indeed."

"So, um, what kind of guys is she into...?"

"...Excuse me?" Kuroe, her expression blank, tilted her head in response to Mushiki's bashful inquiry.

"Er, maybe that was a bit too personal. Okay. Um, what sort of foods does she like, then...?"

"No, that wasn't the issue." Kuroe stood up straight, and keeping her eyes fixed on Mushiki, she asked, "Is that really the first thing you want to ask? I'm sure you must have other, more pressing questions, no?"

"I guess so... But, um, still. *Is* it okay for me to ask about that kind of thing? It's probably, like, secret, right...?"

"Why are you beating around the bush at a time like this? Please don't hold back. First things first, I want you to understand the situation in which you find yourself."

"A-ah, well, in that case..." Mushiki cleared his throat, and his cheeks having turned slightly red, he asked, "Um, so about her *body measurements...*"

"That isn't what I meant," Kuroe interrupted him. "Are you a simpleton? Or is that you in there, Lady Saika, and you're just playing games with me? Surely you have more urgent questions in need of answers. *Where am I?* for example. *Why have I become Lady Saika?* That sort of thing."

"Ah, now that you mention it... What's happening to me?! What the hell is going on here?!"

"..." Now that he had started asking what seemed like earnest questions, Kuroe's mouth tightened into a thin line. "Allow me to start at the beginning. As I said earlier, you're currently inhabiting the body of Lady Saika Kuozaki, the world's strongest mage and the head of this mage training school, Void's Garden."

"Yes. Ah, no matter how many times I hear it, it's such a lovely name..."

"...I would have expected the word *mage* to have been the part to catch your interest."

"Ah, sorry."

As Kuroe said, that was indeed an intriguing word. Mushiki's apology was wholehearted. "So by *mage*...you mean someone who can cast spells? Like hurling fire or healing allies or something?"

"That's a rather abstract impression, and dare I say it, a few generations out of date, but yes."

"Seriously? You're saying mages really exist?"

"Can you explain what has happened to your body through other, more conventional means?" Kuroe countered.

"...I suppose not," he found himself answering. As the saying went, the facts speak for themselves.

He could certainly think of no other way to explain how he, Mushiki Kuga, had somehow been transformed into a girl named Saika Kuozaki.

"I know you must have your doubts, but for the time being, let's proceed under the assumption that magic *does* exist."

"All right... So what's going on with my body?" Mushiki asked in a meek voice.

Kuroe lifted a finger into the air, placed it firmly against his chest, and said, "I'll start with the conclusion. You and Lady Saika have *coalesced* into a single body."

"Wha—?! B-but that's...!"

"I understand it must be difficult to remain calm right now, but I must ask you to please refrain from—"

"Aren't you supposed to get married before doing that...?!"

Kuroe closed her eyes for a moment. When she finally opened them, her expression seemed to suggest that she was taking in some repulsive sight. "You may have Lady Saika's body," she said, "but perhaps I'll have to knock some sense into you?"

"I'm sorry. That word, it was just so, so *stimulating*..." Mushiki shrank back.

Kuroe, regaining her composure, continued: "Mushiki, wasn't it? According to your story just now, Lady Saika was fatally injured when you found her last night, yes? It's only natural, then, to infer that someone must have attacked her, wouldn't you say?"

"Right... Any idea who it could have been?"

"I'm afraid not."

"So there wasn't anyone who had a bone to pick with her, then?"

"I would say she had as many enemies as there are stars in the sky."

"..." Hearing her put that so bluntly, Mushiki felt a cold sweat building on his forehead.

"Nonetheless," Kuroe continued, "there shouldn't be anyone capable of killing the strongest mage in the world, the Witch of Resplendent Color, Saika Kuozaki."

"..."

Those calmly spoken yet resolute words forced Mushiki to catch his breath.

"My apologies. Let's continue." Kuroe must have noticed his reaction, as she stopped to clear her throat. "I suspect that, in all likelihood, your assailant and Lady Saika's are one and the same."

"Right... I thought so, too."

Mushiki's thoughts took him back to those final moments.

That ruthless blow that had felled him as he had tried to save the blood-soaked Saika.

He might not have been able to see his attacker's face, but the wound left on his body had been all but identical to that on Saika's.

"You were both on the verge of death and would in all certainty have truly died had not Lady Saika, drawing on the last of her strength, made use of her final magic technique."

"Her final magic technique... What's *that* supposed to mean?" Mushiki asked.

Kuroe raised her right and left index fingers, slowly bringing them together until they touched. "A fusion spell. It's simple addition. Left alone, you would have both died. So it was better that at least one of you survive. $0.5 + 0.5 = 1$. Lady Saika, on the brink of death, found you, also about to breathe your last, and merged the two of you into a single being in order to extend your life span."

"*Merged*," Mushiki repeated softly, his voice filled with shock as he raised a hand to his cheek—although all things considered, he wasn't even sure if it really was *his* cheek anymore.

"Yes. Hence the word *coalescence*."

"...So you're saying there's nothing left of *me*, then...?"

"Perhaps the injuries dealt to Lady Saika's body were less severe, or it may have had something to do with the amount of magical energy latent in the two bodies. I can't say... It would appear, however, that Lady Saika's body is serving as the base. Having said that, please don't be alarmed. This doesn't mean your body has been lost forever, simply that the parts of you that have been fused are now hidden. I suspect that, in all likelihood, your body is supplementing Lady Saika's injured one."

"Huh? But—"

"I understand you're in shock, but please, wait till I finish explaining—"

"Am I really worthy of this honor...?"

"...Could you please, just for a moment, stop trying to make me feel like an idiot for attempting to help you here?" Kuroe said, her stare piercing Mushiki.

Mushiki did realize he was being somewhat unreasonable, and he did his best to apologize.

"...Now then, from what I can see, that body is entirely Lady Saika's. However, the mind, I take it, is wholly yours, Mushiki?"

"Ah..." His breath caught in his throat.

It did seem to be that way.

If his consciousness had merely been swapped with hers, that would mean that his own body must be somewhere out in the world with Saika's mind.

Otherwise, if his body had simply been transformed into a copy of hers, that, too, would suggest that the real Saika must likewise be out there somewhere.

If what Kuroe said was true, if the two of them, both on the verge of death, had fused into one so as not to perish, then there could only be the one of them.

"So Saika's mind...her soul... Where did it go...?" Mushiki asked, his voice shaking.

Kuroe, after a short pause, slowly shook her head. "I don't know. She may be dormant inside your body. She may have become a wandering spirit, drifting somewhere far afield. Or maybe..." She didn't finish that thought.

It was just a possibility, but even so, it was no doubt too awful to put into words. Mushiki didn't press further.

"...In any event, we need to discuss what to do from here. We're in a state of emergency. It's no exaggeration to say that this is the greatest crisis the world is facing at this present moment," Kuroe said, her expression grim.

Mushiki couldn't help but feel doubtful. "The world...? I mean, sure, losing a beauty like that *is* a huge deal, but even so... Huh?"

As he spoke, an alarm began to sound throughout the school building.

The next moment, a girl's voice blared out from a PA system: "*This* is Erulka Flaera. We have confirmed the deployment of an annihilation factor, estimated yield between calamity- and war-grades. Time for reversible annihilation is two to four hours. Knight Anviet Svarner has been assigned to respond. Everyone, maintain a state of heightened vigilance."

"...? What's all that supposed to mean?"

"Hmm." Kuroe held her chin in one hand for a moment before glancing back at him. "This is a good opportunity. Let's go outside. It's time you saw the other side of our world for yourself."

After exiting the headmistress's office, Kuroe led Mushiki to the rooftop of the central school building.

Before stepping out, she had made him leave behind the slippers he was still wearing and change into proper shoes. The heels might have been relatively short, but being unaccustomed to them, his gait was a little wobbly.

"Come along, this way. There are some steps here, so please do be careful," Kuroe said, holding out her hand.

"Sorry," Mushiki replied, accepting her support as he took a somewhat long stride. "Is this...?"

Arriving at the rooftop, Mushiki made his way to the tall fence at its edge, raised a hand to keep his hair from being buffeted by the wind, and turned his gaze to the scene unfolding below.

He could see far into the distance, with a much wider field of view than he had had on the ground.

Centered around the school building was a vast site containing several additional facilities, all surrounded by a high wall. Beyond those fortifications was an expansive cityscape.

"Ah... So it's just a regular city, huh."

"Yes. Perhaps you're wondering where we are?"

"Well... When you mentioned magic, I kinda assumed I had been whisked off to another world or something."

"You've been unaware of our presence, but we've long been operating in the shadows. This Garden is located in the eastern part of Ohjoh City."

"It's closer than I thought... But I don't remember ever seeing anything like—"

"That's because we've erected a field around it, which serves to keep us under the radar of outsiders... Now, I would like you to please stop staring at the ground below and pay attention to the sky above us."

"Huh?" As instructed, Mushiki looked upward.

At that very moment, the tranquil clouds floating above broke apart, and *it* appeared.

"...? What is...*that*?"

That was a claw—an enormous claw tearing through an empty sky.

No, *empty* wasn't quite the right word—rather, a fissure seemed to have torn through space itself, a great crack ripping through the firmament.

That wasn't all—that fissure was growing increasingly larger...

The next moment, as though cleaving the heavens in two, a gigantic shadow reared its head.

"What...?" Mushiki's eyes opened wide in alarm.

Its massive body was covered in what looked like a tough hide, its arms and feet each equipped with talon-like claws, while long horns sprouted out of its head and a pair of wings emerged from its back.

It almost reminded him of an ancient dinosaur—or maybe a giant monster from a sci-fi film.

"Annihilation Factor No. 206: Dragon," Kuroe said practically in response to his thoughts. "With its tough and unyielding body and its tenacious spirit, it won't fall to anything but the strongest of attacks. Its fiery breath could turn all of Japan into a sea of fire in a matter of days. It's a relatively common form of an annihilation factor," she continued, her tone of voice indifferent.

As though in perfect sync with that explanation, the dragon let out a tremendous roar before spewing out a violent torrent of smoldering flames.

"What...?!"

The sky above burned with scorching heat, and though those flames remained a long distance away, they were powerful enough to make his skin feel like it, too, was on fire. He could barely even keep his eyes open.

With that ferocious fiery breath, it was like a scene from some ancient myth.

What on earth would become of the people, the fields, the cities lying in its path?

The answer to that question flashed in front of him.

"...!"

In the blink of an eye, the landscape before him was engulfed in flames, the familiar cityscape, his home until just yesterday, transformed into a blazing inferno.

Flames swept across the ground, along the streets, painting everything before him in shades of black and red.

There were screams. Alarms blaring. Sounds of destruction. All of it mixed together, all of it sweeping through the whole area.

For a moment, his mind was unable to process the sheer scale of the destruction, and he could do nothing but watch in quiet dismay.

"What...? Um..."

After a few seconds, his brain finally freed itself from its stupor and began to take in the situation, passing orders to his arms and legs.

Desperately, he grabbed the shoulder of the young woman by his side. "Kuroe! The city!"

"I can see. Please calm down, Mushiki."

"You expect me to *calm down* at a time like this?! How are *you* able to watch with such indifference?!"

"Because panicking will not improve the situation. Besides..." With Mushiki still shaking her shoulders violently, she pointed at the sky. "If you don't pay attention, you'll miss it."

"...Huh?"

Mushiki followed her finger, his gaze turning upward once more.

At that moment—

"Yeeeaaahhh! Yahoooooo!"

* * *

A loud cry rang out, and a small shadow took off from the ground like a bullet being blasted up into the air.

They soared in a straight line, struck the dragon like a bolt of fierce thunder, and sent its huge body tumbling across the sky.

"What...?"

The dragon's deafening howl was powerful enough to send shock waves through the air.

That wasn't an attempt to make its presence known, nor to intimidate its enemies—rather, it was a cry of tremendous pain and grief.

"You're a pain in the ass, you oversize lizard!" With those words, the figure who had sent the dragon flying spread their arms wide.

Then something like a small satellite circling through the air exploded with light.

The next moment—

With an incredible detonation like a nearby thunderstrike, the sky was engulfed in a dazzling glow.

Mushiki had to cover his eyes in the face of that blinding flash.

"...Ugh!"

When he could finally open them again, the humongous dragon had vanished, gone without so much as a trace.

"Wh-what was that...?" Mushiki stammered.

"Knight Anviet Svarner. He's a cornerstone of Lady Saika's chevaliers and an S-class mage at the top of the Garden's ranks. I had little doubt he would be able to handle an annihilation factor of that level by himself," Kuroe answered, still staring at the sky.

"Lady Saika's chevaliers...? You mean, she's even stronger than him?"

"It's ridiculous to even compare them," Kuroe answered coolly.

"...Whoa..."

Dumbfounded for a moment, he breathed a sigh of relief before lowering his gaze.

"Right, the city—"

He cast his gaze back to the sea of flames that had engulfed the cityscape—but found himself at a loss for words.

"Eh...?"

The source of his surprise was simple. Until just a moment ago, the city had been enveloped in bright-red flames, screams erupting all around—but now it had returned to normal as though nothing at all had been amiss.

"Huh...? But the whole city was on fire just now..."

"Indeed. That was no illusion. The city had certainly been devastated by the dragon's flames. Had Anviet not defeated the monster, what you just saw would have been the *result* laid down in the history of the world."

"...So you're saying that since the dragon was defeated, it never actually happened?"

"To put it simply, yes. Those who dwell outside the Garden won't remember it all," Kuroe said matter-of-factly.

Mushiki could only stare out at the city in shock, hardly able to believe what he was hearing.

Slowly, the dribs and drabs of information that Kuroe had offered him began to fall into place.

"Are you saying this kind of thing happens often...?"

Kuroe gave him an exaggerated nod, her gaze unflinching. "This was the fifteen thousandth one hundred and sixty-fifth occurrence."

"Eh?"

"That is the total number of times that mages, starting with Lady Saika, have saved the world."

"...! B-but that's...?!"

"Yes... The world faces an annihilation event roughly every three hundred hours, on average."

"..." Mushiki could only stare back at her, his incredulity plain to see.

"It isn't only dragons. There is the fruit of wisdom with the power to create star- or planet-destroying weapons, psychic anomalies that bring about endless natural cataclysms, swarms of golden locusts that devour everything in their path, deadly pandemics with massive fatality rates, emissaries from the future hoping to change the course of history, and a gigantic conflagration that would encompass the entire planet with its mere existence... These entities, each of them with the power to destroy the earth as we know it, we call *annihilation factors*."

She paused for a moment before adding: "The work of mages like us is to use our skills to eliminate those annihilation factors. In the past, there have even been one or two such events that only Lady Saika herself was capable of resolving. Do you understand what I'm saying? If not for her, this world would have surely been destroyed. *That* is how vital the person with whom you have merged is." She spoke quietly as she told him this, but there was an unmistakable zeal to her voice.

Mushiki's hands were trembling as he took in this shocking revelation. "I-it's unbelievable...," he whispered under his breath.

Kuroe forced her eyes shut. "Indeed. Your apprehension is understandable, but I assure you, it's all true."

"Hold on. You said there's one of these *annihilation events* every three hundred hours, and there's been more than fifteen thousand of them now...? So counting back, that means she's been doing this for more than five hundred years, right...? And she's still got such beautiful, silky skin... Yep, it's unbelievable, all right..."

"..." Wordlessly, Kuroe unleashed her pent-up fury.

"Ow, that hurts! Stop!" Mushiki was forced to lift his hands over his head in an attempt to shield himself from her repeated strikes.

The next moment—

"...! Eh?"

Like a meteor hitting the ground, a flash of light touched down before them as a man appeared.

"Yo, Kuozaki. So you were watchin' from up here, huh? Must be nice livin' it up."

The man was young and, though slim, had a well-toned, muscular body adorned in a well-tailored shirt complete with a vest and slacks.

He had tan skin, and his black hair was tied back in a braid. He had the sharp eyes of a predator, and a wild smile stretched across his face. Altogether, his appearance reminded Mushiki nothing short of a ferocious animal.

"You're..."

There could be no doubt about it. He was the mage responsible for crushing the dragon just now.

As proof of that, two vajras—golden weapons shaped like claws—floated in the air beside him, crackling with electricity.

Moreover, there were two huge wings at his back, shining like halos. That divine aura was an odd match with his otherwise wild appearance.

With Mushiki staring back in stunned silence, the man's lips puckered as he flashed them a bold grin. "Somethin' up? You look like a pigeon shot dead by a peashooter. Ah, maybe you've been wowed by my awesome magic techniques, eh?" the man said with a flippant shrug.

Mushiki found himself nodding along. "It *was* awesome. That was *you*?"

"...Hah?" The man's mouth dropped open, his confusion obvious.

"It was amazing... Such a huge dragon. You must be an incredibly strong mage... Right?"

"Hah...? Wh-what're you blabberin' about...? Did your breakfast disagree with you or somethin'...? And there's somethin' up with your voice, too..." The man pulled back, almost flinching.

Despite his words, however, his cheeks had turned a light pink.

"No. I said it was amazing because it *was* amazing. I mean, how did you *do* that?"

"*H-how...?* I mean, it wasn't all that hard, just my second substantiation, you know...? I—I guess I *did* tweak the formula a little, though."

"I see! Your spell... I don't really understand it. What was it exactly?"

"Like I'm gonna tell! Why do I gotta share my secrets?!"

"Don't say that. Come on. I just want to know how you pulled off that awesome move. Tell me."

"...F-fine... I guess I can show you a little...," the man mumbled, his lips slowly curling into a grin.

As scary as he might look, he didn't seem all that complicated.

"You'll do it?! Thank you! Um..."

"Hmm?"

"Did you mention your name just now?" Mushiki asked lightheartedly.

At this, Kuroe let out a small sigh that all but said *This is bad*.

The man had seemed somewhat relaxed up till now, but with this question, veins began to throb on his forehead. "H-hmm...? So that's it...? Basically, I'm just a small fry, not even worth rememberin'...?

"Huh? N-no, not at all. I just had a bit of a mental block for a moment—"

"Fine! I'll just have to drill it in you till you never forget the name Anviet Svarner again! Arggghhh!"

Anviet (right, that was his name) flared with anger and stomped his leg heavily on the building rooftop.

As his boot made impact, a burst of terrible lightning exploded in all directions.

"...?!"

A net of light crisscrossed the rooftop like a spider's web—and before he knew it, Mushiki found himself petrified.

"Hold on...! Stop!"

"Shuddup! If you're gonna beg for your life—"

"What if Lady Saika's beautiful face ends up getting scratched?!" Mushiki cried out.

"..." Anviet's cheeks twitched. "I guess there's no need to hold back, huh...?!"

With that, he lowered his hands—and the two vajras floating around him began to rotate at incredible speed, glowing as they charged with electricity.

"Take this! Vajdola!" As he cried out, Anviet thrust his hands forward and unleashed his ultimate attack.

Mushiki's vision was flooded with blinding white light.

"...What?!"

He swallowed his breath, his stiffening body practically pinning him down.

"Mushiki!" Kuroe cried out, followed by a deafening roar.

He was perfectly aware that he had to try to dodge this attack, and yet his body refused to move.

Violence so overpowering that not even reason could stand up to it. A primitive, instinctual urge to survive. Even to Mushiki, who didn't understand the first thing about magic, it was clear as day that this would be a fatal blow. Soon that raging golden lightning strike would tear his body to pieces.

That said—

"..."

What dominated his mind wasn't fear or despair—but a curious sense of unease.

The burst of electricity that should have rent his flesh apart was moving strangely slow, as though time itself had somehow drawn to a halt.

Yet in this slow-motion world, his thoughts continued to turn at the same pace as before. It was a transcendental experience.

Was this what it meant to see your life flashing before your eyes as you approached death?

It was said that, at the moment of death, the human brain starts to think at an incredibly high speed, sorting through its prior experiences in the hope of finding a way out. As a result, time seems to move more slowly.

Nonetheless, it was all well and good for his brain to be dredging through his past memories, but there was nothing in there that would help him get out of *this* situation.

Don't be afraid. You have the strongest body in the world now.

...

"Huh?"

Out of nowhere, a voice had echoed in his head. Mushiki's eyes widened in alarm.

It was faint and distant but too clear to be an auditory hallucination. But what on earth *was* it?

Strangely, the moment he had heard it, an eerie sense of peace washed over him.

Something told him that it was the same voice he had heard before passing out the night before, the voice of his first love.

Your body remembers how to use its powers. Trust it.

"..."

At that moment, Mushiki raised his hands in front of him.

Not even he properly understood what was driving his actions. Nonetheless, he was sure this was the right course of action.

A heat was building up inside him, as though the blood running through his veins was warming up.

Soon a glow filled his field of vision, enveloping numerous thunderbolts, while above his head, radiant rings of light came into being.

One by one, they came together to form something resembling an angel's halo, while at the same time, others joined vertically—almost like a witch's hat.

"...*Four* points?!" Kuroe's awestruck voice echoed behind him.

In an instant, space began to bend and warp around him—*and the world was transformed.*

That wasn't metaphor or hyperbole.

Until that moment, Mushiki, Kuroe, and Anviet had been standing on the rooftop of the central school building.

Yet a split second later, everything around them had changed— replaced by a blue sky extending forever into the distance.

That wasn't all. Mushiki looked down below and took in both earth *and* sky.

On the ground was a vast urban cityscape, and in the sky, a similar metropolitan scene, only upside down.

It was familiar—and yet at the same time uncanny. The tips of so many tall buildings and radio towers were pointed downward straight at them. All in all, it reminded Mushiki of the jaw of a huge beast.

Then Anviet's panicked voice rang out. "A fourth substantiation...?! Hey, Kuozaki! No fair! That's a forbidden—"

Before he could finish his sentence, Anviet's cries were cut off then and there.

The cityscape below had begun to rise, or perhaps that above had begun to fall, both coursing toward him as though to rend him to pieces.

"...The creation of all things. Heaven and earth alike reside in the palm of my hand. Pledge obedience—for I will make you my bride." Though he was only half conscious, those were the words that emanated from deep inside his chest.

Anviet, still hoping to resist, lifted his arms to the heavens—but the lightning that he summoned scattered without effect.

"Ngh...?! D-dammit! Aaauuuggghhh!"

Like a bamboo boat being thrown about by the waves, poor Anviet was consumed by the gaping maw of those towering edifices.

The world was progressively losing its form.

Yet a few moments later, everything returned to normal, with Mushiki and the others back on the rooftop of the central school building. The rings of light that had appeared over his head were also gone.

The only difference was that Anviet was now lying flat on his back.

His high-quality shirt and slacks were stained and torn, barely maintaining their function as articles of clothing. His long hair was covered in dirt, his body riddled with cuts and bruises. Nonetheless, his limbs were twitching at odd intervals, so he must have still been alive.

"What was all that...?" Mushiki stammered in a daze, glancing down at his hands as he clenched them into fists over and over. Those thin and beautiful fingers moved in accordance with his will.

He didn't have the faintest inkling of what he had just done.

Still, he understood that the inexplicable scene that had unfolded in front of him had been the result of his own power.

It was an indescribable feeling, unlike anything he had ever experienced before.

A burning sensation, as though his blood was at a boil as it flowed from his brain to the ends of his fingertips.

A sense of elation, as if his very existence had swelled like an inflating balloon.

Most of all—a sense of omnipotence, as if he could fit the entire world into the palm of his hand.

This strange concoction of impressions struck him all at once, leaving him momentarily stunned.

"D-damn you...!"

"...!"

Anviet's resentful voice, trickling from a body still lying flat on the roof, pulled Mushiki back to the present.

"Um, are you okay...?" Mushiki approached, crouching down to check that the man was all right.

Anviet, for his part, struggled to raise his face, until his bloodshot gaze landed on Mushiki. "I-I'll remember...this... I'll...kill you, y-you—"

Nonetheless, he wasn't able to complete that sentence, as Kuroe trampled his face underfoot.

"Gyargh!"

At once, he fell motionless. Not even his limbs, until now twitching slightly, still moved.

"..."

It didn't look like she had intended to silence him—or even to deal the finishing blow. If anything, it might have simply been an act of carelessness as she approached Mushiki.

"Kuroe?" he called out to her.

Her expressionless countenance was the same as ever—other than that, she was unable to contain a shred of astonishment, mixed with the zest of excitement.

"...I can't believe it. Even with Lady Saika's body, for you to perform a fourth substantiation like that... But this could only mean—"

No sooner did she begin to mutter under her breath than she cut herself off, glancing back his way. "Mushiki."

"Y-yes?" Feeling pressured by her intense stare, he could only nod in uncertainty.

"It's unfortunate that you find yourself dragged into all this," she said. "Even so, I must ask you for your help. The fate of the world rests on your shoulders."

"Uh, I'm not really cut out for all that...," Mushiki answered.

That was to be expected. He was just an ordinary high school student. What was *he* supposed to do if called upon to save the world just like that?

"..." Kuroe scowled, making him break out in a cold sweat. "Is this not one of those situations where you should just *go with the flow?*"

"All the same..."

She stopped for a moment to ponder before continuing: "With your cooperation, we may be able to find a way to separate you and Lady Saika. Should that effort prove successful, I would be happy to introduce you to her anew, as someone to whom we all owe our lives."

"What have I got to do? I was just thinking I was in the right mood for a little world-saving," Mushiki blurted out.

Kuroe fell silent, breathing out a resigned sigh. "We need to make the necessary preparations. But we should deal with a certain contentious issue first."

"A certain *contentious issue?*" Mushiki repeated blankly.

Kuroe responded with a single nod.

Around thirty minutes after the scuffle on the roof, Mushiki was led to a large set of doors inside the central school building.

"What's this, Kuroe?" he asked.

"The conference room. The Garden's management department is holding its regular meeting today... Given the circumstances, I would prefer not to attend, but it would be out of the question for Lady Saika to not be present." Kuroe paused there before coming out with a warning: "The management department and various knights should already be inside. I will deal with them as best I can, so please keep any comments to a minimum."

"All right. We can't ruin Lady Saika's image, right?"

"Yes, indeed." Kuroe's expression seemed to suggest that wasn't what she was thinking at all, but she evidently decided to leave it at that.

She knocked loudly on the door, gradually swung it open, and gestured for Mushiki to enter.

Though somewhat on edge, he did as she instructed.

"Whoa..."

The moment he stepped inside, Mushiki let out an audible gasp, despite already having been warned to keep silent.

He couldn't help it. There were already close to ten figures in the meeting room, and they each rose to their feet to welcome him.

"Lady Saika. Please take a seat," Kuroe urged in an attempt to break through his stupor.

Right, he couldn't just stand there in the doorway forever. He made his way awkwardly to the large table and sat himself in a vacant chair.

When he did, the others in the room, still standing, gave perplexed looks.

"M-Madam Witch...?"

"Is everything all right...?"

"Huh...?"

Mushiki looked on quizzically, when Kuroe approached from behind. "Lady Saika's seat is over there," she whispered, pointing to the place at the head of the table.

The seat of honor. Although given the room's unsettling atmosphere, it seemed more like the place where the boss of an evil organization might sit.

"Ah..." He rose to his feet and hurried to reseat himself at the right position.

Only then did the others sit down.

"..."

Well aware of a strange tension that had fallen over the room, Mushiki glanced around at the other members.

Then he slightly frowned. Most of them were dressed in tidy suits, but two were clearly out of place.

One was a girl who seemed to be in her early teens, though her firm eyebrows and slightly reddened cheeks made her look even younger. She was wearing a long white robe, but for some reason, beneath that, she

was clad only in a top and a pair of skintight leggings like something from a tribal costume. It almost looked like casual underwear and was a complete mismatch in comparison to the rest of
the members.

"...Kuroe, who's that?" Mushiki asked in a small voice.

"Knight Erulka Flaera," Kuroe whispered. "She may look young,
but she's the second longest-serving mage here at the Garden after
Lady Saika."

"Oh..."

As the saying went, you couldn't judge a book by its cover. Mushiki
was struck with wonder.

Next, his gaze turned to the girl sitting directly across from him.

She, too, looked young in years, though not quite to the same extent
as Erulka—sixteen or seventeen years old, if he had to guess. She
was dressed in the same uniform as the other students he had seen
outside.

Her hair was tied back into two long pigtails, her eyes were a lovely
almond shape, and her thin, well-defined lips told of great strength
of will...

At that moment, Mushiki stopped.

Her face—he had seen it somewhere before.

"...It can't be... Ruri?" he murmured.

"...Yes? What is it, Madam Witch?" responded the girl, her head
cocked to one side. She was clearly elated to have been addressed
directly by the esteemed Lady Saika.

"Er... It's nothing," he murmured softly.

He hadn't meant to call out to her, but she had clearly heard him.

Out of the corner of his eye, he could see Kuroe staring at him in
suspicion.

He could hardly blame her. After all, he had suddenly called out the
name of someone whom he wasn't supposed to know.

At that moment—

"...!"

Just as he was wondering how he could brush this all off, the doors to the conference room slammed open, and a man, covered from head to toe in bandages, staggered inside.

At first, Mushiki wasn't sure who he was looking at, but when the newcomer gave him a piercing glare, he knew—it was the knight he had fought just a short time ago, Anviet Svarner.

The various faces of the management department stared at the knight wide-eyed.

"Kn-Knight Svarner! Your injuries...?!"

"Don't tell me they're from your fight with an annihilation factor?!"

"Impossible! For Anviet, an S-ranked mage, to end up like this?!"

Anviet clicked his tongue to silence the flustered onlookers. "Shud-dup. As if I would ever lose to a drip like that."

"B-but your injuries...?" a man wearing glasses asked—to which Anviet fixed Mushiki with a hateful glower.

At this, the other faces assembled each let out understanding sighs.

"...So it was Madam Witch."

"Ah, I suppose it can't be helped, then."

"You're lucky to be alive, Anviet."

"Don't just nod your heads, you bastards!" Anviet grunted as he threw himself down in the seat beside Erulka.

He must have been in considerable pain, as his body was trembling and his face was twisted in a grimace...but he clearly didn't want the others to realize just how bad a condition he was in, as he didn't make so much as a noise.

"You're late, Anviet," Ruri said, glowering. "What do you have to say for yourself, making Madam Witch wait?"

"...Shut up. Just be grateful I'm here at all," Anviet snapped back.

Ruri shook her head, then turned her gaze back to the others assembled around the table. "In that case, now that we're all here, let's begin. The first item on our agenda today is..." As she spoke, she reached out to the computer terminal in front of her and projected an image over the center of the table. "Since our last briefing, there have been two annihilation events: a number five hundred and eleven, a leprechaun, and a number two hundred and six, a dragon. Both were successfully subdued within the window for reversible annihilation. Injuries sustained by our mages..." In a loud, clear voice, she moved on from one item on her report to the next.

Mushiki couldn't really follow everything she was saying, but he knew that it wouldn't be appropriate to let his boredom show. As such, paying constant attention to his posture and deportment, he resolved to listen along with all due diligence.

After Ruri had finished, several others had reports of their own to share.

"Thank you, all. Does anyone else have anything to add?" Ruri asked roughly forty minutes later once everyone had spoken, glancing around the room.

The assembled members responded with silence.

Perhaps sensing the strained atmosphere, Ruri gave them all a single nod. "In that case—"

But at that moment, Kuroe, until now standing behind Mushiki's back, stepped forward. "Excuse me. Might I be permitted to make an announcement?"

"And you are?"

"My apologies. My name is Kuroe Karasuma, Lady Saika's attendant. Lady Saika permitted me to attend today on account of her ill health."

"What?!" Ruri exclaimed in response to this. "I-ill health?! I-is she okay?!"

"Yes. There is no need for concern. Is there, Lady Saika?" Kuroe's gaze all but impelled him to play along.

"H-huh? Ah, r-right." Mushiki nodded.

"So? What did you want to say?" Erulka asked, chin in hand.

Kuroe gave a nod of assent. "Yesterday, Lady Saika was attacked by an unknown assailant. We suspect they were most likely a mage, but we haven't been able to confirm their identity. It's possible they might try to strike again, so we would like to request a strengthening of the security net."

"...?!"

The faces of everyone gathered stiffened.

"Wha—?! M-Madam Witch was attacked?!"

"And they managed to get away without being identified...?!"

"Th-that's not possible!"

The members of the Garden's management department were visibly shaken.

To be honest, so was Mushiki.

Lowering his voice, he whispered: "Is it really okay to tell them that, Kuroe?"

"There should be no issue so long as we keep Lady Saika's present state under wraps. Rather, this should ensure that they remain more vigilant from now on," Kuroe said flatly while observing the panic of the others present.

Mushiki nodded in understanding. Right. If they said nothing, his assailant could try to strike again while he was still vulnerable.

"Bah! Ha-ha! Ha-ha-ha!"

In the midst of that great confusion, one voice broke out into laughter—Anviet's.

"You're sayin' you let an enemy knock you for a loop, *and* you let 'em get away without even figurin' out who they were? Ha! Disgraceful! I guess our good old Madam Witch has gotta be feelin' her age, huh?" he scoffed with an exaggerated shrug.

At this, Ruri, who until that moment had been watching Mushiki with concern, turned to Anviet with a scowl. "You've got a big mouth today, Anviet. *You* can hardly talk, seeing how many times you've lost to Madam Witch yourself. Isn't that right?"

"Hah...?" One eyebrow twitching, Anviet glared back at her.

Yet Ruri sought to fan the flames further. "This mysterious assailant couldn't be *you*, could it? Did you finally realize you're no match for her and so decided to ambush her in a sneak attack?"

"Haaah?! Wh-why, you—"

"Oh, my apologies. I let myself get carried away just then. There's no way *you* could be the attacker... If *you* had tried anything, she would have turned the tables on you before you could so much as bat an eye!"

"I'll kill you, dammit!"

"Bring it on!"

Anviet and Ruri both jumped up from their seats so fast that they sent their chairs flying.

All at once, the room was filled with an oppressive air, light itself whirling around the two opposing figures.

Nonetheless—

"Silence! Fight on your own time!"

Erulka, seated between Anviet and Ruri and clearly irritated, slapped the both of them with the sleeves of her long robe.

"Ngh..."

"...Ms. Erulka."

Though reluctant and still on edge, the two calmed down and retook their seats. The various faces of the management department each breathed sighs of relief.

"Very well. We'll make the necessary arrangements... Do you have anything else to report?" Erulka demanded, her eyes locked on Kuroe.

Taking this as her cue, Kuroe added softly: "Lady Saika would like to make a proposal."

"Oh? And what would that be? Speak."

"First, for the time being, she will refrain from responding personally to annihilation events lower than obliteration-grade. She also wishes to reduce the frequency of these regular meetings."

"Hmm... That can be arranged, but why? Don't tell me she was injured in the attack?" Erulka stared straight into Mushiki's eyes.

Mushiki felt his heart skip a beat in the face of that gaze, which seemed to look right through him.

Nevertheless, Kuroe remained serenely calm as she shook her head. "That would be preposterous. Regardless of the opponent, it's unthinkable that Lady Saika would suffer injury."

"I know. I was joking... But why, then?"

"Lady Saika has another matter to attend to."

"What other matter?" Erulka tilted her head quizzically.

With that, Kuroe gave her a single, confident nod before declaring:

＊　＊　＊

"Yes. Starting tomorrow, Lady Saika will be attending the Garden as a student."

"...Huh?"

All those in the room, Mushiki included, were rendered thunderstruck by those words.

Chapter 2
⊷ Garden ⊶

At Void's Garden, the mage training institute located in Ohjoh City in Tokyo, the room for class 2-A was filled with a strange tension.

"…"

The students lined up in orderly rows, along with the homeroom teacher standing by the table at the front, all holding their breaths, their expressions fraught, as though utterly convinced that letting out so much as a sigh might lead to the gravest of consequences.

It called to mind a herd of weak herbivores desperately hiding from a larger predator. Desperately trying to blend into the surrounding landscape so as not to attract the notice of their natural enemies or any transcendental beings. As future mages whose mission would be to save the world from destruction, they looked rather unreliable.

That said, no one could accuse them of cowardice.

Above all—

"Y-yes... Introductions... We have a new transfer student coming to join us today, Lady Saika Kuozaki—er, uh, just S-Saika, I suppose..."

The head of the entire school, and the most powerful mage in the world, the Witch of Resplendent Color, Saika Kuozaki, had unexpectedly joined this class as a transfer student.

"Ah, right. Nice to meet you, everyone."

In appearance, she didn't look much older than the other students. She was a beauty, complete with mesmerizing, lustrous hair. She couldn't possibly be used to wearing her school uniform, but it did look nice on her. If those present in the classroom hadn't known just how significant a figure she really was, they would have no doubt been utterly captivated by her appearance.

However, her incredible, overwhelming depths of magic, the legends of her prowess, were already engraved in their minds, and her shockingly beautiful multicolored eyes didn't allow them to feel at ease.

...Why is the headmistress transferring in as a student...? Wh-what's her goal...?

No way; is she looking for promising students or something...? I'd better find a way to stand out...!

But what if I do something to upset her...?

The unvoiced cries of the other students all but flooded the classroom.

The homeroom teacher in charge of introducing Saika to the class was likewise shaking in trepidation. If anything, *she* was probably the most stressed individual in the entire room.

That was when it happened.

"...Argh, I can't take this anymore!"

Having seemingly lost her patience, a serious-looking girl rose to her feet.

"Wha—?!"

Watching on, the other students, and the homeroom teacher, too, caught their collective breath.

"...! D-don't do it, Fuyajoh! Restrain yourself!"

"Don't make a scene! That's Madam Witch we're talking about!"

"Are you willing to throw away your entire career?!"

Like a dam breaking, voices rose out from everywhere, urging the girl to hold back.

In spite of that, her face awash with resolve and determination, the girl stepped toward Saika.

"Madam Witch," she called out.

"Wh-what?" Saika stuttered.

With a devil-may-care expression, the student pulled out her smartphone. "Can I take a picture...?" she asked, sweat beading on her forehead and cheeks.

At those words, the entire class held their heads in relief, shock, and exasperation.

That girl was none other than Ruri Fuyajoh of class 2-A and the Knights of the Garden, a well-mannered student with excellent grades—and a huge, huge fan of Saika Kuozaki.

"...F-Fuyajoh! Don't be rude! Return to your seat!" Finally, the homeroom teacher, Tomoe Kurieda, rushed in to stop her.

Tomoe was in her midtwenties, around a head taller than Saika in height—but perhaps due to her cowering expression, or her trembling voice, she came across as the younger of the two.

"...Sorry, Ms. Kurieda. I know I'm being disrespectful, but there are times when a woman has to fight, even when she knows she shouldn't...!"

"What's that supposed to mean?! You're making a scene in front of the headmistress here, don't you realize?! Wh-what if it becomes *my* responsibility?!" the homeroom teacher screamed.

The other students looked on, aghast as she let her true colors show, but Tomoe seemed like she didn't notice.

"...Just so I'm clear, what's the worst possible punishment you can give me for ignoring your instructions?"

"Huh? Th-that would be...suspension...I suppose?"

"Hmm..."

"Ah! I know that look! You're thinking you might be suspended, but this could also be a rare opportunity to be chosen as a witch!"

"Don't stop me! It isn't every day you get to see Madam Witch dressed in a school uniform! How will I be able to look myself in the mirror tomorrow if I let this pass?! I need to save this moment for all posterity...!"

"Nooo! I know it sounds nice, but you'll ruin my reputation if you do that!" Tomoe cried, shaking Ruri by the shoulders with tears in her eyes.

Ruri, however, didn't budge an inch. She truly was indomitable.

Watching from the sidelines, Saika gave them both a soft smile. "Ah...it's okay. I don't mind. Take as many as you want," she said with a grandiose nod.

"M-Madam Witch...?"

"Are you sure?!"

"Yep. Saika doesn't often—I mean, I don't often wear school uniforms, so I understand how you feel. We must have similar tastes. I would have taken some selfies this morning myself if Kuroe hadn't stopped me."

"...Huh?"

"It's nothing. Photos, right? I don't mind... Can you send me a copy later?"

"...! O-of course!" Ruri's face lit up, and she quickly held her phone in front of her like a professional photographer, taking picture after picture of Saika from various angles.

"Madam Witch! Please look over there!" she called out in excitement.

Saika was more than happy to oblige, striking an enthusiastic pose. "H-how about this?"

"Yes, I can't get enough of it! Gorgeous! Absolutely beautiful!"

"What about this pose, then?"

"I'm dying! You're killing me, Madam Witch! Incredible! You're a natural!"

"What about one of Saika Kuozaki leaning against the windowsill with a melancholy look?"

"Eeep?! Oh my god...! H-how do you know what I want and dream of...?!"

So in a corner of the room, a full-on photo session had begun.

The most powerful mage in the world, the school headmistress Kuozaki, was posing happily in front of many onlookers—while Ruri, usually so serious and levelheaded, was positively gushing with glee as she snapped one picture after the next.

Utterly bewildered, the other students could only watch as this scene continued to unfold before their very eyes.

"What the hell is going on here...?"

"Is she testing us or something...?"

"The strength of a mage lies in their strength of spirit... Don't let yourself get carried away..."

No, there was no letup at all to their confusion.

Earlier...

"...Er, so can you explain this to me, Kuroe?" Mushiki asked upon their return to the headmistress's office. "Why do I—I mean, why does Saika have to attend the school as a student? Isn't she supposed to be the boss around here?"

Kuroe responded with a nod. "As I mentioned earlier, your present status is that you have merged with Lady Saika."

"Right."

"I would like to separate you both as soon as possible—but that won't be so straightforward. First, we must find a way of dealing with the other facets of this situation."

"You mean the attacker...right?" Mushiki asked.

Kuroe bobbed her head. "From what I understand, the assailant must have caught Lady Saika unawares. If you had been attacked before she had regained consciousness..."

"..." Mushiki felt a cold sweat running down his back.

Needless to say, in that case, he would have died.

If the attacker was to try again now, he would almost certainly be killed.

That would mean the complete and total death of Saika Kuozaki.

"So first of all, you need to be able to control magic yourself, at will. When the assailant shows themselves once more, you *must* be capable of countering them."

"Magic... You can't expect me to pull off what I did to Anviet again. I don't even know *how* I did it."

"Don't worry. This Garden is an institution dedicated to the training of mages well versed in all forms of magic. There is no better place to learn than here."

"Yeah, but this is still so sudden. No matter how much I learn, there's no way I'll be able to pull off what Saika could..."

"By the way," Kuroe interrupted, ignoring the hesitation in his voice, "all students at the Garden must wear the appropriate uniform. They're made from a special fiber, physically and magically toughened by what we call *spirit thread*. At the end of the shoulder straps is something that we refer to as a *realizing device*. Think of it as a wand used by modern-day mages. You should have already seen some of the other students here using theirs."

"...? This is all happening too quickly. It does sound amazing, but still—"

"The uniform will look very good on Lady Saika, I'm sure."

"I'll do it." Mushiki's answer was so fast that he took himself by surprise.

Without even realizing it, he had found himself going along with Kuroe's plan to make him attend this school of magic as a student.

"..."

"What's wrong, Kuroe?"

"...I know I was the one who suggested it, but I do have mixed feelings when these things proceed *exactly* the way I hoped."

"...Well, it's the results that matter," she followed up under her breath. "You will be attending the Garden starting tomorrow, Mushiki. Rest assured, we will deal with your family and your previous school outside the Garden."

"You'll *deal* with them...?"

"Don't concern yourself over them," she said in a commanding tone.

...Well, he would have been lying if he had said he wasn't worried, but he could hardly go back to his old life in his current body. He would just have to leave it all to Kuroe to handle.

"As for your class... Yes, 2-A should be a good fit."

"Based on what?"

"Among the students is a knight, Ruri Fuyajoh. She may be a student, but she is exceptionally skilled—she's one of our leading knights, in fact. You never know when there might be another attack, so it won't hurt to have a powerful mage by your side."

"Ah... So that's Ruri's class? Heh, she was amazing, all right."

"...Hmm?" With him agreeing so easily, Kuroe looked his way quizzically. "Speaking of which, Mushiki, you seem to already know her. Have you met?"

"Ah, right. She's my sister."

"...Hah?"

What followed was a long, drawn-out silence.

Finally, Kuroe let out an uncharacteristic timorous voice. "Your *sister*? Ruri Fuyajoh?"

"Yeah. Well, my parents got divorced a long time ago, and I haven't seen her in years. We pretty much lost all contact."

"...So after seeing your long-lost sister at a mage training institute, that paltry reaction was all you felt...?"

"No. I mean, I'm in Saika's body right now, right? I can't exactly act all surprised and happy to see her again, can I?"

"That's true... Although, I can't quite say whether you were being thoughtful or just *messed up*." Kuroe looked vaguely uncomfortable, but she quickly regained her composure. "In any event, you will join class 2-A as Lady Saika, Mushiki. But first, there are a few things you should be aware of."

"What?" Mushiki wondered.

Kuroe raised a finger into the air. "First of all—you must never let on that you are not, in fact, Lady Saika."

"Ah... Yeah, that makes sense. I don't want to ruin her image or anything."

"That's true enough, but there's another reason, too."

"Which is?"

"There is every possibility that your assailant is already aware of your survival."

"...I see." Mushiki nodded.

The fact that their target, touted as the strongest mage in the world, had escaped through some unknown means and was still alive would be no small matter to the attacker. If they were to attempt to strike again, they would undoubtedly proceed with considerable caution. However long that lasted, it would offer him at least some reprieve.

However, if Mushiki's current situation was to become known, the enemy would strike again without hesitation. After all, he was just an interloper in the guise of Saika Kuozaki. He had no idea where the aggressors might be lurking, so he would have to be immensely careful of what he said and did.

Though, there was one major problem that would have to be overcome.

"I'll make an effort, of course... But I don't really know a whole lot about Saika, do I?"

"I'm aware of that," Kuroe replied, sensing his concern. "I will prepare a collection of videos of her. Be sure to study her speech patterns and mannerisms as much as possible."

"Huh, is that really okay?!" Mushiki leaned forward in excitement.

Kuroe's expression soured slightly. "I don't exactly feel comfortable showing them to *you*... But necessity knows no law. It isn't enough to look like her. You must earnestly *become* Lady Saika."

"You want me to *be* her...?"

"I know it's a lot to ask, and it may be an affront to your own personal dignity. But right now—"

"I'm kinda nervous, y'know?" Mushiki exclaimed, his cheeks turning slightly red.

"Ah yes. I suppose I need to learn, too...," Kuroe said with a stern look. "I know this won't be easy, but we are grateful for your efforts. Now, I'll say this once more—under no circumstances are you to reveal that you are not the real Lady Saika. Understand?"

"Yep, leave it to me. This is all for her." Mushiki nodded strongly.

"..."

Sitting in his seat after morning homeroom, Mushiki silently propped his elbows on his desk and wrapped his fingers around his forehead.

The reason was simple. Even though Kuroe had reminded him just yesterday not to do anything stupid, he had already gotten wrapped up in a photo shoot before class had even begun.

Of course, he *was* trying to be careful. From the minute he had arrived at school this morning, he had been doing his utmost to imitate Saika Kuozaki's mannerisms.

But the moment Ruri asked to snap some photos, he had thought: *I want those photos, too!* Thus, he had let himself get carried away, striking one pose after another. To be honest, even now while reflecting on his actions, he was still looking forward to receiving the finished pictures.

...Hold on. Wasn't Ruri working directly under Saika as her subordinate? In that case, wouldn't Saika herself have found it difficult to turn down her request? If so, maybe he *had* made the right choice? Then again, the amount of effort he had put into getting that final special shot, an image he had already titled *Saika Kuozaki Playing with Her Hair in a Cool Breeze*, had probably been overkill...

"...Or not," he murmured under his breath, stopping himself there.

If left unchecked, the small voice inside his head might start a full-blown analysis of Saika's behavior to justify his actions.

He had a few things to reflect on, but it was also very much unlike Saika to dwell on the past. What mattered to her was the future. Keeping that in mind, he decided to fix his sights on what was ahead of him.

"Madam Witch!"

A familiar voice caught his attention.

"Ah, Ruri," he answered, turning toward her as she placed something down on his desk. "What's this?"

"The photos I took a short while ago! You said you wanted them, so I had them printed as fast as I could!"

"Ah. That *was* quick." Mushiki feigned calm as he picked them up.

Inwardly, he wanted to jump to his feet in joy, but he had to hold it in.

"Yep! The portable wireless photo printer is one of the seven indispensable tools of a modern maiden! I printed them under my desk while the teacher was talking!" Ruri puffed out her chest in pride, her eyes twinkling.

"Ruri...," called out a new figure suppressing a smile as she appeared behind her. "Homeroom is an essential part of the Garden curriculum, you realize? Besides, you shouldn't bully the teacher so much."

Mushiki turned his gaze to a kind-looking student dressed in a Garden uniform, her carefully braided hair reaching down to her shoulders. Her brow was creased in a frown, as though expecting trouble.

"Yeah, of course. I know," Ruri responded nonchalantly.

The girl remained at a visible loss. "Ah... I know, and that's just the thing... How many times have I warned you? But getting Madam Witch involved, that's, well..."

"But she's in a school uniform, you know? I'll say that again—she's in a *school uniform*. This could be a once-in-a-lifetime miracle, you know? Did you hear me? Do you need me to repeat myself?"

"I—I heard you... I can see how enthusiastic you are about it..." Faced with Ruri's impassioned remarks, the girl took a step back.

Watching on, Mushiki found himself letting out a small laugh. "I'm sorry. It looks like I've caused you a little trouble. Um..."

"Ah...! M-my apologies! I'm Hizumi Nagekawa. I'm in the same dorm room as Ruri here," the girl introduced herself, hurriedly bowing her head.

Mushiki gave her a light nod. "You don't need to stand on ceremony. I'm not the headmistress here, just a fellow student. Rather, I'd be grateful if you could teach *me* while I'm here."

"O-of course..." Hizumi shrank back in reverent fear.

Observing from the side, Ruri puffed out her cheeks.

"Ruri?" Hizumi asked.

"I can help her."

"Huh?"

"Sure, you're a good teacher, but you know? I can help Madam Witch, too! If you want, I'll stick by your side and support you for your entire academic life!" With a huff, she turned her face away, sulking.

"Come on, don't pout. I'm counting on you as well, Ruri," Mushiki said with an awkward chuckle.

Something about her behavior reminded him of the past.

Thinking back, how many years had it been since he had last seen her? In his memories, she was still a small child. Her hair, too, had been much shorter than it was now.

He never could have imagined he would meet her again in a place like this—and he in a different body no less...

"...Madam Witch? Is there something on my face?" Ruri asked, staring back at him strangely.

His emotions getting the better of him, he must have been staring at her for an uncomfortably long time.

Mushiki shook his head. "No, no. It's your hair. I just thought it looks wonderful. It was nice short, but long hair suits you, too."

"Oh..." Ruri fell silent, her cheeks flushing. "You're a smooth talker, Madam Witch. Yes, I used to wear it shorter, but my brother told me once that he likes girls with longer hair, so I grew it out..." She stopped there, as if just realizing something. "Huh? Madam Witch, did I show you a picture of when I had shorter hair or something?"

"A-ah," he stuttered.

Now I've done it.

Apparently, that was something Saika shouldn't have known.

Though it would be even more out of character for Saika to rush to make things right after a mistake like that, so ignoring his pounding heart, he gave Ruri an elegant wink.

"Heh. I know everything about you, Ruri, you know?"

"Oooh!" Ruri clutched her hands to her chest, as though the wind had just been knocked out of her.

Then, staggering, she propped herself upright with one hand on the desk and struggled to breathe. "M-Madam Witch... You almost had me swooning there..." She wiped her mouth with the back of her hand.

Hizumi, visibly anxious, feigned a chuckle.

Thanks in part to Ruri's own response, it looked like he had managed to cover his mistake. Mushiki breathed a sigh of relief, glad the two girls hadn't seen through him.

◇

"The second point to note is the proper handling of magical energy."

Earlier, back in the headmistress's office, Kuroe had continued her second round of explanations.

"The proper handling...of magical energy? I don't even know what that means..."

"Think of it as the latent energy that resides in all living things. Broadly speaking, it can be divided into two rough categories—the external energy that fills the world and the internal energy that exists within each individual. The former is known as mana, the latter as od." Accentuating each point with hand gestures, Kuroe carried on: "I won't go into the details now, but Lady Saika's internal life force energy far surpasses that of most average people. That is to say, using her power, she can activate techniques of a scale that would be beyond ordinary mages, unless of course they drew on external energy, too."

"Wow. Saika sounds incredible, wouldn't you agree?"

"Yes. She is incredible. But right now, that enormous reservoir of magical energy is like a waterfall spilling out of control... Can you see anything around your body?"

"...?" Mushiki glanced down at his hands.

As he strained his eyes, he couldn't help but feel as if his surroundings were somehow vaguely aglow.

"Whoa... What's going on?"

"That is Lady Saika's magical energy. You must have only become aware of it after I mentioned it to you."

"Huh? Is it that easy to see?"

"Hardly. It usually takes a student close to a full year to develop an awareness of someone's magic. Don't forget that you are looking through Lady Saika's eyes right now." After a short pause, Kuroe cautioned, "Remember that a powerful mage has already detected your innate magical energy. Lady Saika's assailant may believe her dead, so they may not be keeping an eye out for her...but the situation won't remain this way forever."

"Right... So it won't be good if she keeps on leaking it all over the place, huh?"

"Indeed, though I'm a little concerned about how you phrased that... First, you must learn to feel—no, to *remember*—how to hold your magical energy inside your body."

"Remember, huh?" Mushiki crossed his arms at this odd usage of words.

"Yes. Just as you have now remembered how to sense magic, that ability likewise lies latent within Lady Saika's body. However, because you don't know how to activate it, it isn't working. What you need is awareness and recognition... You should also know that magical energy is a powerful force in and of itself. Even without casting spells or techniques, simply gathering it in your hand and throwing it at a target can be particularly destructive. Especially when we're talking about Lady Saika's magic, the most powerful on earth..."

With an almost threatening tone, Kuroe concluded: "Please do be careful."

Unsurprisingly, the atmosphere in the classroom remained unchanged when it came time for their first-period lecture.

Though, strictly speaking, it seemed to have become even more strained than during homeroom.

" ... "

The other students didn't look at Mushiki unkindly, but he could sense that they were all paying keen attention to his every move. If he was to so much as sneeze, he suspected, some of them might even be thrown from their chairs in shock.

" ... "

Feeling ill at ease, he let out a short sigh.

Then Ruri, in the seat beside him, spoke in a voice just loud enough that only he could hear. "Don't let them get to you. They're all just nervous." Her words were accompanied by a soft smile.

Incidentally, Ruri's seat had been a good distance away earlier in the day, but for some reason, she seemed to have moved right next to him by the time class began.

The student who had originally been at the table next to Mushiki's was now sitting in Ruri's old seat, her body visibly quivering. Just what kind of *negotiation* had Ruri imposed on her?

"...Ah. I know. It just feels so strange. Like their gazes are reaching out and stroking my body all over."

"Well, there's nothing we can do about it. I mean, you're so dear to us all, Madam Witch. How could we *not* be intrigued by you?"

"Right... I suppose *reaching out and stroking my body all over* might not be the best way to put it, either? But it makes your heart race a little, don't you think?"

"Huh? Did you read my mind just now?" Ruri's cheeks turned red, her eyes widening.

Mushiki suspected that he knew why everyone seemed to regard her as a genius.

"Well, er... We should probably all get a grip and move on to today's class," said their homeroom teacher, Tomoe Kurieda, at the front of the room, her tone suggesting she was still in fact far from doing that herself. It looked like she would be responsible for first period.

As her trembling fingers reached out to the wall, a dim light appeared. It seemed to be some kind of electronic blackboard.

Each desk was equipped with a modern, even futuristic-looking tablet-style terminal—a far cry from what Mushiki would have imagined he might find at a so-called magical academy.

Speaking of which, he had asked Kuroe about that, but her response had been one of utter confusion. "Why would you use magic when electricity will suffice?" That simple reply had left him at a loss for words.

"So let's continue where we left off yesterday, on the topic of the Five Great Discoveries and Transformations in the history of magic..." So Tomoe began the lesson, her fingers shaking slightly as she manipulated the digital blackboard.

For their part, the students turned down to their tablets to take notes while still stealing furtive glances Mushiki's way.

"...As you all know, the history of magic can be roughly divided into five distinct generations," Tomoe said. "These are the discovery of magic, the application of spells and techniques, the use of magic circles and diagrams and their application to matter—"

"...Hmm." As he listened to the lesson, Mushiki stroked his chin.

Not surprisingly, he couldn't understand a word she was saying.

Nevertheless, he couldn't afford to let it go to waste. After all, not only his life, but Saika's, too, was at stake here.

So while he felt a little guilty about interrupting the lesson, he raised his hand. "Um, can I...?"

"...!"

At that moment, every set of eyes in the classroom locked onto him.

The situation was already nerve-racking, but this only further added to the oppressive tension. The students' expressions seized up.

What on earth could the headmistress have to add here? That was the question on everyone's minds as they stared his way with bated breath, unable to move so much as a muscle.

"Kyargh! D-d-did I overlook something...?!" Tomoe stammered, her shoulders heaving as though she was about to break down in tears.

Mushiki felt sorry about having to ask this, seeing how she looked like an abandoned dog left shivering out in the rain, but he could see no other way.

"Um, no, I just have a question, that's all."

"A-ah... Wh-what is it...?" Tomoe asked in unfeigned terror.

No doubt everyone would laugh when they heard it, but he asked anyway. "Sorry for asking something so basic, but...can you start by explaining briefly what magic is?"

"...?!"

The class was in shocked silence at Mushiki's question before quickly being gripped by an uproar.

"...Wh-what magic...*is*...?"

"She can't mean that... It might sound simple, but it's a terrifyingly deep question...!"

"A philosophical proposition seeking to understand the very basis of magic... You might as well ask *What is a human being?*...!"

"That's the kind of curveball you expect at an academic conference or something! This isn't beginner's territory!"

"Watch out, Ms. Kurieda...! If you slip up before Madam Witch..."

The murmurs of the other students, having read far too much into Mushiki's question, buzzed throughout the room. They all meant to keep their voices down, but he could make out everything they were saying.

He couldn't tell for sure whether Tomoe, too, had heard them, but regardless, her face turned an almost sickly purple.

She seemed to fall to pondering before answering, but eventually, sweating buckets, she pressed her head down against the lectern.

"...I—I— I'm s-s-sorry, Madam Witch...! I'm just a shallow instructor, without the training to answer your profound question...! P-p-please spare me...!"

"I just want a normal answer," Mushiki responded, scratching at his cheek.

She stole a few furtive glances his way before finally raising her face, awash in fear. "J-just a normal answer...? Really...?"

"Yes. Like I'm a beginner."

"A-all right..." Still seemingly at a loss, she launched into an explanation. "M-*magic* is a general term for techniques that rely on using magical energy to cause various phenomena... There are several different types of magic, but here at the Garden, we focus on the most common ones used to bring about physical substantiations... Th-that's right, isn't it...?" Tomoe asked aloud, glancing anxiously toward the students.

You've got this, their expressions seemed to say as they nodded back at her. *Good luck!*

" ..."

Mushiki continued to stroke his chin. To be honest, he still didn't understand.

"Can you explain how it's done, though? Just a really basic answer will be fine."

"Huh...? W-well..." Tomoe slowly lifted a hand into the air and raised her index finger. "The first thing I learned a long time ago now was to move your finger and try channeling your magical energy through it... It's easier if you think of it like collecting cotton candy around your finger...," she said, still twirling her finger in the air.

Looking carefully, Mushiki could see that a small layer of light did indeed seem to be gathering around it.

"Hmm."

Right. He, too, should be able to pull off that much, at least. Kuroe had also told him that he ought to be able to so long as he knew the process.

Following Tomoe's example, Mushiki extended his own finger and spun it through the air, envisioning a ball of cotton candy.

A split second later—

Poof! A huge mass of cotton candy came into being right then and there!

It continued to grow—until it soon grazed Tomoe's hair and shot through the digital blackboard, blasting away the walls, the floor, and the ceiling.

"Heh?!"

Just like that, a gaping hole opened up at the front of the classroom. The electrical wiring running through the walls and ceiling must have been damaged by the explosion, as electricity was pouring out in sparks. At the same time, a breeze blew in from outside, catching a piece of Tomoe's hair that had been cut off by the explosion and sending it fluttering through the room.

"...Wow..."

Startled, she was unable to let out so much as a scream. Her eyes rolled back into her head, and she fell to the ground like a puppet whose strings had been cut.

"Ms. Kuriedaaa?!"

"You *did* ask her to start with the basics...!"

"Please contain your anger, Madam Witch...! Ms. Kurieda never meant to insult your intelligence...!"

With the teacher having collapsed, the other students, initially

watching in shocked silence at the sheer suddenness of the situation, started crying out at the top of their lungs.

Amid them all, only Ruri by Mushiki's side sat with her arms folded, nodding in admiration. "Raw magical energy. I'd have expected no less from our Madam Witch. A sound reminder not to get overly fixated on any particular spell or technique, no matter how complicated it might be. I'll engrave this lesson into my heart."

Ruri's voice was filled with unshakable confidence, but the other students, aghast, kept glancing between her and Mushiki, their expressions all but saying *Wh-what's that supposed to mean...?*

"..."

Of course, he hadn't meant anything of the sort. It was an accident; that was all.

However, he couldn't let people think the most powerful mage in the whole world would make such an elementary mistake.

"...Hmm. Keep working at it, everyone, you hear?"

Fighting to calm his racing heart, feigning composure, Mushiki came out with his best imitation of the Witch of Resplendent Color.

...This mission of his, he realized, would be considerably harder than he had imagined.

After lunch break, it was time for fifth period.

Mushiki was on his way with his classmates to the training hall, a huge structure on the western side of the Garden.

It was a vast field in an unfamiliar design, surrounded by an array of machines and tiered grandstands below a retractable ceiling. It looked more like a sports stadium than a gymnasium, similar in a way to the Colosseum of ancient Rome.

It was a magnificent and grandiose facility, and under any other circumstances, Mushiki would have stood in awe at its center, marveling as he took in his surroundings.

He did not, however, do that. He had two reasons.

First, it would have been out of character for Saika.

Second, he was preoccupied with something else.

"Ooh... I see... What do we have here...?" he murmured, staring down at himself.

Yes. Fifth and sixth period were practical lessons, so he had changed into his sports uniform for ease of movement.

A short-sleeved top, sports leggings, and shorts. While light in weight, they seemed to be made from the same material as the Garden's school uniforms and, consequently, were quite tough.

At first glance, this sports outfit wouldn't have seemed a good fit for Saika's mysterious demeanor. Even so, the mismatch between clothes and personality seemed to bring out a hidden charm in her that Mushiki had never even imagined. If he was being honest, he already rued the fact that there wasn't a mirror in the immediate vicinity.

As these thoughts swam around in his head, he heard a choking sound coming from behind him.

"...! Madam Witch in gym clothes...?! C-can this really be happening...?! This is like a one-of-a-kind, limited-edition piece of merch! I-I've gotta snap pictures while I still can...!"

This, of course, was Ruri. She was wearing the same type of gym clothes, and her eyes were swirling in delirium.

She gestured as though to take yet more photographs, but her hands were empty. Her face awash with regret, she slammed her foot down hard on the floor of the training hall. "Ugh... Where's my camera when I need it?!"

"Didn't you leave it in the locker room...?" responded Hizumi, standing behind her, scratching at her cheek.

"Why would I have done that?!"

"Because we're doing a practical class, right...?"

As Ruri and Hizumi continued to debate the whereabouts of the camera, a man, his gait languid, came from the back of the hall.

"Huh...? Get your asses in line, kids," he said with a sleepy yawn.

Mushiki looked at the newcomer, and his brow rose in surprise.

It was Anviet Svarner, the same knight who had confronted him yesterday. During times of peace, he apparently worked as a teacher.

Mushiki had no idea how, but it looked like his injuries were completely healed. At the very least, there was no sign of the bandages that had covered him from head to toe the day before.

Instead of yesterday's slacks and vest, he was now garbed in a sports tracksuit, black in color and decorated with gold lines. That said, he was wearing more accessories around his neck and wrists than Mushiki could count, so he didn't exactly look to be dressed for exercise.

"Let's get crackin'. We'll start with some warm-up exercises, then move on to practicin' some basic substantiation techniques..." Anviet's voice trailed off as he glared at Mushiki. "Eh? What the hell are *you* doin' here, Kuozaki? And dressed like a student? What're you playin' at this time?"

Before Mushiki could reply, Ruri stepped forward with her hands on her hips. "Oh, have you forgotten our meeting yesterday? It *was* brought up. Starting today, Lady Saika will be attending school as a student."

"Hah? She was *serious* about that? What the hell? *Why?*" Anviet asked with one eyebrow raised.

Mushiki, maintaining his composure, fixed him with a complacent smile. "Ah... I've been feeling a little sluggish lately. I thought I might try doing a little training to regain my bearings. This way, I can get a firsthand look at how the students are doing. And also..." He paused for a second, flashing Anviet a wry grin, before continuing in a dramatic tone: "And also, it will give me an opportunity to inspect the teaching staff. We have to make sure they're all up to par, don't we now?"

"...*Huh?!*"

Mushiki could clearly see a vein throbbing on Anviet's forehead.

Well, that was understandable. After all, he had just implied that Anviet wasn't quite up to snuff as an instructor.

The result of this declaration, however, was as he expected.

According to Kuroe, Ruri had no objection whatsoever to Saika's course of action. Erulka had likewise shown her understanding. Anviet might have been somewhat affronted, but it was nothing that couldn't be brushed over with a little delicate manipulation.

"Fine, then. But you had better make sure there's no misunderstandin' about your position now, you hear me? Whatever your reasons, you're a student at the Garden, right? We don't tolerate students mouthin' off at teachers, do we?"

"What...?! Anviet, you don't mean to...?!" Ruri broke into a frown at this provocative assertion.

Mushiki raised a hand to restrain her and said with a soft smile, "Hmm, I see. I apologize. Mr. Svarner?"

"..."

This condescending yet fearless tone only served to make Anviet's face flood with even greater anger. To be honest, Mushiki *was* somewhat on edge facing off against Anviet's intimidating personality.

Saika, however, wouldn't have been—and so he did his best to conceal just how nervous he actually was.

"...Good. If you're gonna do this properly, I'll play ball," Anviet finally responded, before following up with a backward glance over his shoulder as he left for the other side of the hall. "Don't blame me if you can't keep up, though!"

Then, at the other students who had been watching nervously, he shouted, "What the hell do you think you're lookin' at, punks?! Get on with those exercises!"

"Y-yes!" the students answered in unison, quickly lining up and beginning their warm-ups.

It looked like there was a fixed routine. Mushiki did his best to imitate the others' movements.

It wasn't long before Anviet's infuriated voice rounded on him again: "Put some effort into it, Kuozaki! Stretch out those tendons! It's sloppiness that gets you hurt out there in the field!"

"Huh? Ah... Sorry." Mushiki did as instructed, stretching the tendons in his legs.

Then Anviet howled further instructions: "Three laps around the track when you're done! And don't slack off, you hear me?!"

"Ah...? *Three* laps?"

He had expected something more unreasonable, given that this was supposed to be a thorough workout. He was almost disappointed.

Yet Anviet strolled right up to him before barking in an almost cartoonish manner: "Are you a dumbass, Kuozaki? These're just warm-ups. I thought it was common sense that pushing yourself too hard puts a greater strain on your body. You *are* a teacher, aren't you? We're tryin' to improve the *quality* of your exercises, not the *quantity*. So pay attention to your stride and the swing of your arms, dammit!"

"A-ah..."

Strange though all this felt, Mushiki still ran around the track with the other students.

Perhaps sensing his mood, Hizumi appeared beside him with a forced smile. "Ah-ha... Mr. Anviet might look scary, and he does have a rude way of speaking, but he knows what he's talking about..."

Then, her expression placid, Ruri said, "He's actually pretty serious. He might not like you, Madam Witch, but he won't single out any of his students for punishment. So he isn't all that bad."

"..."

Those comments did change Mushiki's impression of Anviet, albeit only a little.

In the meantime, the students had reached the end of their jog and were gathered together in the center of the training hall.

Anviet stood in front of them. "Should be all warmed up now, I'll bet. Let's get started, then." So saying, he let go of a small, metal ball-like object.

A dim light spilled out from it, seemingly solidifying into a pair of legs springing up and down on the ground. It looked like a mobile target. Was this also some kind of magic? It was a mysterious technology, that was for sure.

"*You* first, Fuyajoh."

"Yes."

Ruri stepped forward. Perhaps she was following Mushiki's lead, or maybe she was usually more disciplined, but her tone was now slightly politer than it had been earlier.

"After you, Madam Witch."

"Ah. I'll see how you do it first," Mushiki answered.

Ruri's cheeks turned slightly red, and she pumped her arms, raring to go. "All right, then!"

She narrowed her eyes, holding her arm outstretched as though to concentrate.

"Senjitsu Fuyajoh, Second Substantiation: Luminous Blade."

The very next moment—

Two glowing patterns unfurled above Ruri's head.

Her *world crest*. Similar patterns of light appeared whenever someone was using a magical substantiation technique.

It was the same phenomenon as the halo that had shone over Saika's head or the one on Anviet's back. Ruri's, however, was more like a valiant helmet—or the face of an angry demon.

Her hand, still outstretched, began to glow—and then a long weapon-like object appeared in her grip, forming a *naginata* comprised of shimmering light.

Ruri swung it around, adopting a defensive stance.

"…"

Mushiki was momentarily stunned by this fantastic sight.

Yesterday, he had witnessed for himself Anviet's second substantiation and Saika's fourth one.

This, however, was his first time calmly observing the process as a third party.

"I'm ready," Ruri whispered softly.

In response, Anviet snapped his fingers, and the ball waiting in front of them began to run at high speed, its luminous legs stretching and contracting.

As fast as it was, it would be difficult to catch in a photograph, let alone hit with an attack.

Ruri remained unfazed, her gaze sharpened, until—

"…Ah…"

Letting out a short exhale, she drew her *naginata*.

The blade's trajectory carved a long crescent moon.

A second later, the ball, sliced clean in half, fell to the ground behind her with a heavy thud.

It was a perfectly honed, impeccably precise strike.

"Wow...," murmured the remaining students after a moment's pause.

"Hmm. I guess that earns a passing grade," Anviet said, folding his arms as he let out a small sniff.

"Thank you," Ruri responded, letting her *naginata* dissipate into thin air. "Knowing you, I was a little worried you might only appreciate an unnecessarily flashy attack."

"Hah?" Anviet knit his brows.

At that moment, Hizumi quickly gave her a nudge in the ribs, and Ruri, taking the hint, fell back.

"Tch... Fine. You're up next, Kuozaki. I don't know what you're playin' at, but think of this as a chance to show these kids what our vaunted headmistress can pull off," Anviet said, releasing another of those small metal balls.

"Oh, no, I'm..."

Mushiki had to come up with some quick excuse to sit this one out.

What other choice did he have? Earlier in the day, he had practically destroyed the classroom just by gathering a small amount of magical energy. There was no telling what might happen if he, unable to properly wield Saika's vast reservoir of magical powers, was to try training for real here.

"..."

The students continued to stare at him silently. He shook his head slightly... He was a little worried he wouldn't be able to pull it off, but it wouldn't be like Saika to shrink from a situation like this.

"Ah... Right. I'll give it a shot, then."

He feigned confidence as he took a step forward.

He kept his gaze lowered, trying to conjure up in his mind something based on what he had learned from Kuroe last night, similar to whatever technique he had pulled off against Anviet the other day, or the trick he had just seen Ruri perform.

A new technique—a substantiation magic. The art of giving form to the intangible. At its most basic, substantiation magic...was like forging an image by molding a clay of magical energy.

He wondered how he knew that. This was supposed to be his first time attempting it, yet the actions felt surprisingly familiar to his hand.

Regardless, he would have to be careful. If he overdid it, he could end up with a repeat of what had happened earlier in the classroom.

He focused on keeping the output only at the bare minimum, quiet, small, and safe. As he visualized that image at the tip of his little finger—

"—?!" Mushiki's eyes shot open, and he stared up into the air.

Only then did he realize that both Anviet and Ruri had circled around to position themselves in front of him.

Both were breathing heavily, their faces slick with perspiration.

...Almost as though confronting a powerful opponent.

That wasn't all. Anviet's double halo hovered behind his back, while a pattern resembling a demonic mask had fallen over Ruri's face. In one hand she clutched a *naginata*, in the other, a trident.

Their second substantiations. Whatever it was, these two knights, supposedly among the strongest in the entire Garden, were ready for battle.

"Um..."

Not knowing what was about to take place, Mushiki stood there motionless, watching as a bead of sweat coursed down Anviet's chin.

"...K-Kuozaki, you... What're you about to do there...? You're not gonna blow up the whole training hall—heck, the whole Garden—are you...?!"

"Huh...?"

The next moment, Ruri fell to the ground quickly and knelt in front of him. "I-I'm so sorry, Madam Witch...! I never should have pointed my blade at you...! M-my body acted on its own...!" With those words, she bowed her head in deep supplication.

"No, I mean..."

Mushiki didn't know exactly what was going to happen, but he *had* been about to do something.

But how was he supposed to respond to *this...*?

"...Hmm. A prompt reaction. I would have expected no less from you both...I guess?"

Well aware that this was nothing more than a half-baked excuse, he decided to praise the two knights for their rapid responses.

Well, Ruri seemed to take his remarks at face value, but Anviet continued to watch him out of the corner of his eye.

"..."

...He could hardly believe it. Even after trying so hard to suppress his powers, had he really posed such a profound danger? As he glanced down at the slender white hands that were now his own, Mushiki was made acutely aware of the sheer magnitude of power he had now acquired.

$$\Diamond$$

His fifth- and sixth-period classes both proceeded smoothly without incident.

That said, at Anviet's insistence, Mushiki had been forced to observe the remainder of both classes without participating himself.

He had no intention of complaining. In fact, he was secretly grateful.

After all, he still hadn't yet fully grasped how to use Saika's surplus magical energy. Being able to watch how the other students used their magic was invaluable time spent.

For the students as well, it seemed to have been good motivation to have the headmistress observing so closely. It may ultimately have been entirely coincidental, but Anviet had ended up creating the best situation for everyone.

"All right. Let's go, Madam Witch, Hizumi," Ruri said with a stretch of her arms after the teacher had left.

Mushiki, watching on from a seat in the hall, nodded in response as he rose to his feet. "Oh-ho... It isn't often that I get a chance to see a class like this up close. It was rather stimulating."

"Ah-ha... I was pretty nervous, actually. I can hardly even remember what I did..."

"Oh? What a waste. It isn't every day that we get to show Madam Witch our magic abilities."

The three of them continued to chat as they made their way to the locker room at the side of the training hall.

At that moment—

"...Ah."

Upon entering the women's locker room, Mushiki stopped dead in his tracks.

Several of his classmates were already inside, and more than half of them had already stripped down to their revealing underwear.

"...!"

His heart skipped a beat as he cursed himself for being so careless.

It was only natural when you stopped to think about it. Mushiki's body was now that of a woman, and so he was obliged to use the women's locker room. And locker rooms, after all, were essentially places to change clothes.

It was precisely because he understood this basic fact that he had only entered it during the break before fifth period after making sure everyone else had already finished.

Chatting with Ruri and Hizumi, however, he had completely overlooked it. Or perhaps he had let down his guard, what with the day's classes now being over. Regardless, this bountiful rose garden of young ladies now spread out before him, leaving him momentarily at a loss.

"Ah... I feel more tired than usual today..."

"I guess. But it's an honor. To think, we've gotten to see Madam Witch up close like this."

"Don't you think he was kind of cute all flustered like that? Mr. Anvi, I mean?"

"Tell me about it. There's a theory, you know? They say men who act tough are the most vulnerable when others turn on them."

"Ah. Can you lend me your deodorant when you're done?"

"Mm-hmm."

And so on...

Those young maidens continued talking while half naked seemingly without a care in the world.

Their breasts and buttocks, normally shrouded in a realm beyond sight, were now lined up before him, covered only by the thinnest, most unreliable pieces of cloth.

"…"

While he may have fallen in love at first sight with Saika's wondrous form, that certainly wasn't to say that he didn't have feelings toward other women. Not at all.

Alas, such was the nature of the male animal. The soft, silky skin of young maidens, their delicate voices, their enrapturing scents were paralyzing stimulants to Mushiki's brain.

"…? What's wrong, Madam Witch?"

"You look awfully pale…"

Ruri and Hizumi, realizing that something was amiss, called out to him in concern.

"A-ah, no, I mean…"

Mushiki shook his head, hoping somehow to be able to brush this off.

But while he stood there frozen, the two other girls looked to have begun changing their clothes directly in front of him.

The two of them, like the others, had removed their gym clothes, essentially stripping down to their underwear.

"…"

For a long moment, all he could do was stare.

Ruri was his little sister. They had bathed together when they were kids. There was no way on earth she could have caught his interest, not even in her underwear—or so he had thought until just a few moments ago.

Here she was in the flesh, her lustrous, glamorous appearance, unseen now for many years, striking him with an unexpected vividness.

She was wearing a matching bra and panties, pale blue in color and simple in design. The body behind those articles of clothing had an air of sophistication, as though nothing at all was superfluous about it.

She was a warrior, and she was a young woman. The two opposing elements coexisted in her slender body. Mushiki found himself catching his breath.

Hizumi's gorgeous silhouette struck a sharp contrast. Gently wrapped in her warm-colored underwear, she was endowed with weapons of mass destruction that normally dwelled unseen beneath her uniform or gym clothes.

Dressing slimmer—that legendary term from a most ancient document—sprang to mind. Someone who looked slenderer in certain articles of clothing than they truly were. Such was Hizumi's harmless features and her sensational, sensual form. Together, the two sent Mushiki's brain spiraling into the depths of chaos.

This won't do. Nope, not at all.

He could feel himself breaking into a sweat. With his heart already racing from the unexpected shock of seeing everyone else here, this addition could prove lethal. He would never have thought that the sight of his acquaintance disrobing could affect him to this degree. He would have to find some way to regain his composure, or else—

"...?! H-huh...?"

At that moment, he felt his body heating up.

For an impossibly long second, he wondered if he was feeling dizzy from excitement—but he was wrong.

This sensation, as if the very blood in his veins was on fire, was—

"...!"

Driven by an unspeakable sense of urgency, he dived for the door at the back of the locker room and slammed it shut with all his might.

He couldn't say precisely why, but something told him that he couldn't afford to remain there with the others.

It looked like he had jumped into the shower room. There were several showers lined up in a row by the wall, separated by simple partitions and doors with wide openings at the top and bottom.

He wasn't sure whether anyone used those showers after their practical lessons or after working up a sweat playing sports, but regardless,

he didn't see anyone else in the room. For the time being, he heaved a sigh of relief.

"*Madam Witch?! Are you okay?!*" Ruri's panicked voice sounded from the other side of the door.

That was to be expected. After all, from where she was standing, it looked like Saika had suddenly decided to hole herself up in the shower room of all places.

"A-ah... Don't worry about me. I'm just..."

No sooner did he start trying to peddle yet another excuse than he became quiet.

His body, he realized, was letting out a soft glow.

"Wh-what...?"

Unable to process what was happening to him, his eyes opened wide in alarm.

After a few seconds, it seemed to gradually subside, and the burning sensation coursing through his flesh likewise faded into memory.

As far as he could see, at least, nothing serious seemed to have happened. Relieved, he lifted his hands to his chest. However—

"Wh-what the heck...?"

As he murmured under his breath, he was struck by a tremendous sense of discomfort.

The voice emanating from his own throat had turned into something unfamiliar—and at the same time, *all too* familiar.

"...?!"

Choking on his words, he glanced down at his hands.

No...

Those weren't Saika's beautiful, slender fingers, but the rugged, bulky digits of a young man.

On top of that, those magnificent breasts that had formerly graced his chest were nowhere to be seen.

"It can't be..."

After a quick survey of the area, he ran to the wall to catch a peek of his reflection in one of the slightly elevated windowpanes.

"..."

When he saw the face staring back at him, he was rendered speechless.

Of course he was. Because in his reflection, staring back at him with a look of utter bewilderment—was Mushiki Kuga himself.

"...Me...? B-but why...?"

Yes. The long bangs hanging over his forehead, the somewhat blurred impression of his eyes, his pale white skin.

This was unmistakably him before merging with the mage Saika.

Right, Kuroe had said something along these lines. That the two identities were in a state of coalescence, and that Saika was merely the more dominant at the present moment.

Although for this transformation to have taken place so suddenly...

"Oh..."

At that moment, Mushiki had a fit of recollection.

Kuroe had given him a final point of caution the previous night.

"Now then, the third and final thing to note..."

In the headmistress's office on the top floor of the central school building, Kuroe raised a third finger into the air and suddenly fell silent.

She remained that way for a long time, as though carefully pondering her next words.

"...Hmm? The third point?"

"...No, never mind. You'll probably be fine."

"What? You can't not tell me now. You've got my full attention."

"It might be best not to worry about this one. After all, it will be difficult to develop appropriate countermeasures regardless... Very well. In the event that something happens, I'll step in directly, so don't concern yourself about it," Kuroe said flatly.

Mushiki, let down by this response, puckered his lips. "You aren't saying this on purpose to *make* me worry, are you, Kuroe?"

"Don't be absurd," she answered, her knowing eyes avoiding his gaze.

"No way. She couldn't have meant *this*...?!"

Except he could think of no other explanation. It was certainly true that this was beyond *countermeasures*, and if he had known in advance, he might have acted strangely from sheer fear... But even so, if something like this could happen, he ought to have been given *some* warning!

"*Madam Witch! Madam Witch! Are you okay?! I'm coming in!*" Ruri continued to shout as she knocked on the door.

"...?!"

Mushiki's shoulders quivered with fear.

This was the shower room inside the girls' locker room. And right now, he was a man.

There was no way he could let anyone walk in on him like this.

"Hold on," he cried back without thinking. "I'm okay, so don't—"

"*...?! Whose voice was that?!*"

"...Uh-oh."

He covered his mouth with his hands, but by then, it was already too late.

He could hear a commotion breaking out among the girls on the other side of the door.

"*Eh...? Huh? Was that a* man's *voice...?*"

"*But Madam Witch just went in there, didn't she?*"

"*Was he lurking in the shower room before we came in...?!*"

"*A high-level pervert?!*"

"*Maybe Madam Witch noticed that sick freak and decided to deal with him herself!*"

"*I'll help you, Madam Witch...!*"

"*J-just gimme a minute to put my clothes on...!*"

All of a sudden, the locker room was abuzz.

Mushiki let out a strangled cry, his throat constricting.

He couldn't let them find him like this. But there was no way out other than going through the locker room. The window at the end of the shower room was certainly too small for a man of his size to escape through.

"I-I'd better call Kuroe—"

"You wanted to see me?"

"Wha—?!"

At that moment, the window rattled open, and Kuroe poked her head through.

In response to the sudden appearance, Mushiki fell over, landing hard on his buttocks.

"Owww..."

"Do be careful. Right now, your body is also Lady Saika's," Kuroe said as she twisted and turned through the window until she had fully entered the shower room.

She had a slender build, but it was clear now that she was also unexpectedly dexterous. Mushiki felt like he was watching an acrobat at work—or maybe an escaped fugitive.

"I came as soon as I sensed a disruption in your magical energy. So you *have* undergone a state conversion..."

"A *state conversion*? Wh-what's that supposed to mean...?"

"Let's save the detailed explanation for later. Right now, we need to deal with the situation at hand," Kuroe said, drawing close to him.

Come to think of it, she *had* said she would step in directly should anything happen.

"Is there any way out of this? Please, you have to—"

Mushiki clammed up before he could finish his sentence.

Kuroe had pushed him up against the wall, pressing her hand against it next to his face.

"Um, Kuroe...? What are you...?"

"Be quiet. Your hands are flailing about—no, maybe your mouth?" So saying, Kuroe grabbed his chin with her free hand—and without stopping, she brought her face even closer.

Her nose, her cheeks, even the soft graze of her breath.

Mushiki's heart skipped a beat at the sight of her fine skin, those jet-black eyes that seemed to draw him in, those long eyelashes that filled his field of vision...

"Kuroe, hold on—"

"Ngh..."

As though to completely silence him, she pressed her lips against his own.

A soft touch. The sound of that slightly moist contact. That numbing aroma. All at once, an unstoppable assault overran his body and mind alike.

"..."

For some reason, in his confusion, the memory that stood out most to him was the kiss he had shared with Saika that night.

"Madam Witch! Are you okay?!"

Ruri, wearing her gym clothes backward, stormed through the shower room door.

Behind her, Hizumi and their other classmates peered in anxiously. They might not have deployed their magic crests, but they were all ready for battle.

Ruri had meant to barge in as soon as possible, except that Hizumi had begged her to at least put her gym clothes back on before knocking the door down. Now she scanned the entire shower room as though attempting to make up for the delay.

"...Huh?" she gasped as she took in the scene in front of her.

The only other person in the shower room was Saika, still fully dressed.

"Madam Witch...? Wasn't there a boy lurking in here...?" Ruri asked.

"...Hmm? What are you talking about? There's no one here," Saika answered.

...But how? She felt a little uneasy and tilted her head in consternation. "Um, Madam Witch?"

"What is it?"

"Why *did* you run into the shower room all of a sudden?"

"Oh, that... I thought I had worked up a bit of a sweat; that was all."

"Why are you leaning against the wall, though?"

"Ah... I must have slipped, I suppose."

"...And why is your face so red?"

"That's..." She raised a hand to touch her fingers, then stared back at them. "...a secret, I suppose?"

◇

"It looks like I made it in time," Kuroe murmured after completing the so-called treatment, exiting back through the window she had entered, her skirt now slightly wet.

It looked like it would take some time to dry, but as she had literally crawled out from the shower room, it probably couldn't be helped.

"But to think he underwent a state conversion on his very first day... He'll most likely need further treatment down the road." She stopped and crouched on the ground, covering her face with her hands.

"..."

To any outside observer, it must have looked like she was trying to hide her blushing cheeks.

"...I thought I was prepared for this...but it's still rather embarrassing, when it comes to it...," she whispered, her voice so small that no one could have possibly overhead.

She remained that way for close to a full minute.

"...Well, then."

Having managed to return to her usual expressionless face, she quickly rose back to her feet and sped across the grounds of the Garden as though nothing had happened.

Chapter 3
⊰ Conversion ⊱

Void's Garden could be roughly divided into five main areas.

First came the central area, where the central school building and the headquarters overseeing anti-annihilation factor operations were located.

Next came the eastern area, densely packed with the school's annexes, its medical buildings, and various research facilities.

After that was the western area, largely taken up by most of the school's training facilities and grounds.

Then there was the northern area, most of it off-limits to the general public and that included facilities like the headmistress's residence and several private institutions.

Finally, the southern area was filled with dormitories and various commercial facilities.

Naturally, Mushiki had assumed he would be expected to return to the northern area at the end of the school day.

Nonetheless—

"Kuroe? What is this place?" he asked as he took in the building in front of him.

"As you can see, it's the Garden's first girls' dormitory building," Kuroe answered flatly.

Right. After finishing his first day of classes, he had found Kuroe waiting for him in front of the central school building, and now she had led him all the way to this dormitory in the school's southern precinct.

It was a large, three-storied structure, with an understated yet sophisticated appearance. It looked more like a low-rise apartment building than a student dormitory.

"Unless I'm mistaken, aren't girls' dormitories places where female students live together?"

"Just so. And right now, Lady Saika is both a girl and a student."

"That's true, I guess, but you know... Are you sure you don't have any other reasons for suggesting this?"

"You're very perceptive, Lady Saika." Kuroe, growing weary of this roundabout conversation, continued in a hushed voice: "I won't be able to protect you well in the mansion, Mushiki. In other words, the safest place for you is the same dormitory as Knight Fuyajoh."

"...I see."

Indeed, it would be his residence rather than the school facilities where he would end up spending most of his time at the Garden. No matter how many knights he had by his side during the day, it wouldn't mean anything if he was left completely undefended while asleep at night.

"But won't that pose another problem? I mean, I know I'm now an S-class beauty, the envy of the world, but—"

"There's no need to go that far." Kuroe gave him an unamused look.

"Right," Mushiki murmured. "Still, I'm a guy on the inside. Wouldn't it be wrong for me to stay in the girls' dormitory?"

"I understand what you're saying, but this is an emergency situation. After all, if you should be killed, Mushiki, that would also mean Lady Saika's demise. And her death would mean the end of the world."

"That's...true, I guess, but still..."

Despite saying that, Mushiki felt a sense of unease hearing Kuroe's words.

He understood that if he was killed, Saika would also die. But to him, equating that to the end of the world seemed a bit extreme.

It was true that, without her, the world might face a crisis. Nonetheless, he couldn't help but think that Kuroe had implied just now something much more—that the moment Lady Saika died, the whole world would be destroyed along with her.

"In any event, don't worry." Whether or not she had read his thoughts, Kuroe looked unconcerned and continued: "Usually, we assign two students to a room, but I've arranged for you to have your own private quarters."

"I see. That makes sense."

"You're a man, after all, so there are a lot of things we need to take into account."

"I wouldn't go that far..."

"Oh? Are you saying we needn't worry, then?"

"...I appreciate the concern, I guess..." Defeated, Mushiki averted his eyes.

Kuroe let out a deep sigh and, with a shrug, added: "In that case, follow me."

With that, she led him through the doors of the girls' dormitory.

Though still somewhat nervous, Mushiki followed after her and stepped into this world of women.

First they passed through an electronic authentication system, then into the lobby. The building decor and the facilities were startlingly luxurious for a student dormitory.

"By the way, Mushiki, how was school today?" Kuroe asked in a whisper.

He gave her a small nod. "Right. I was a little nervous, but everyone else seemed even more on edge, so that helped me keep my cool, I think... I'm guessing it will probably take me a while to use magic properly, though..."

"Did you run into any problems?"

"...Um, I guess you could say that..."

"I saw a request had been put in for repairs to classroom 2-A."

"...Yeah. My bad...," Mushiki answered, his gaze fixed on the floor ahead of him.

"..." Kuroe gave him a cold stare.

Despite all that, she had suspected from the very beginning that things wouldn't go entirely smoothly. She let out an exasperated sigh but said nothing more as they made their way down the corridor until she came to a stop outside another door.

"This is your room."

She had led him to a room on the third floor, around ten tatami mats in size and fitted with an extravagant bed, desk, closet, and dressing table all lined up in a row. The overall impression wasn't all that different from Saika's bedroom in which he had first awakened in his *merged* form.

"This is amazing. I know it's a student dorm, but it's so extravagant..."

"The other rooms are fitted with regular furniture. As this will be Lady Saika's quarters for the time being, I arranged to have it properly prepared for her in advance," Kuroe said before motioning to one item after the next. "We've brought you changes of clothes and a number of personal items, though we've kept them to the bare minimum required. If there is anything here that you don't know how to use, please let me know. I'll be staying in the room to your right, number 316."

"Ah. So you're moving into the dorm, too, then?"

"Of course. Taking care of Lady Saika is my responsibility. Just so you know, the room to your left, number 314, belongs to Knight Fuya-joh. In the event of an emergency, she should be able to offer immediate assistance. Now, that's it for our tour. Let's move on."

She opened the door and ushered Mushiki back out into the corridor.

"Where are we going now?" he asked.

"The first floor... In a sense, it would be no exaggeration to say that this is the most important issue for us to address during your stay in the dormitory."

"The most important issue...? Wh-what is it?"

"Look ahead."

As they stepped through the hall—

"M-Madam Witch?!"

"Huh?"

Turning a corner, they came across Ruri and Hizumi coming from the other direction.

Both stared back wide-eyed at this unexpected and sudden situation. Their reactions were understandable, though, seeing as Saika had popped up out of nowhere in the middle of their everyday dormitory.

Ruri turned to Hizumi, her face awash with a look of disbelief. "H-Hizumi. Pinch me. As hard as you can. I'm definitely dreaming here. This is just too unreal. I mean, this is the stuff of love comedies, having the person of your dreams transfer into your class and then start living in your very own dorm, right? At this rate, I'm going to turn into one of those lucky pervert cartoon characters... Hurry...! Before I defile Madam Witch with my thoughts...!"

"C-calm down, Ruri. I can see her, too."

"Ha-ha-ha. There you go joking again." With a dry smile, Ruri pinched herself on the cheek and turned back to Mushiki. "What?! That's the *real* Madam Witch?!" She cried out in astonishment, falling to the ground and landing hard on her posterior.

Mushiki did his best to address her in a refined voice. "Ah, we meet again, Ruri, Hizumi... I'm a student now, you know? So I was thinking I would move to the dormitory for a while."

"R-r-really?! Really?! Wh-which room...?!"

"Number 315."

"Next dooooooor?!" Ruri all but screamed her soul out, collapsing to the floor flat on her back.

Hizumi rushed to her side. "Ruri?! Are you all right?!"

"I—I might be done for... Clearly, I've already received my allotment of happiness in this life... When I die, tell my brother...tell him I lived to the best of my ability...and that I loved him with all my heart."

With that, her strength left her, and she fell limp. Her expression, however, remained one of utmost joy.

"R-Ruriii!" Hizumi cried out as she held her in her arms.

Mushiki, too, was naturally a little worried and looked into his sister's face.

"...Is she okay?"

"Oh, yes. She does this from time to time. She should be back to normal in a little while," Hizumi replied, her voice suddenly collected and cool.

While Mushiki did his best to feign composure, he couldn't help but be a little concerned.

"Excuse me," Hizumi said, grabbing the limp Ruri and dragging her roughly away in a manner that made her look an awful lot like a serial killer disposing of a corpse.

After watching the two disappear into Room 314, Mushiki glanced at Kuroe. "She *is* an S-class mage, right?"

"She is..." Kuroe let out a faint cough in an attempt to collect herself. "Let's continue on. We don't have a lot of time left."

"Ah, right. So what's this important problem we need to think about?" Mushiki asked.

Kuroe gave him a serious look. "The bathing area."

A few minutes later, Kuroe led Mushiki into the changing room adjacent to the large bathroom on the first floor of the dormitory building.

It was an expansive space, lined with shelves along the walls stacked with several baskets. At the back of the room was a row of washbasins—and farther in, a set of large glass doors leading into the bathing area.

"The most important problem...is this?" Mushiki asked in all seriousness.

That being said, it wasn't all that difficult to understand what Kuroe had meant by that. Yesterday, Kuroe had washed him while he had been occupied watching a video recording of Saika to familiarize himself with her character, so this would be his first time properly bathing since ending up in her body.

"Yes. There is a sign out front saying that the bathing area is currently off-limits due to a gas inspection. Let's finish up in here while we still have time. As I'm sure you can imagine, we can't allow the other female students to enter while you're present."

"Ah... Right. I'm glad you thought about all this, Kuroe."

For her part, Kuroe let out a soft snort, watching him through narrowed eyes. "I'm not doing this out of concern for the students. The fate of the entire world is at stake. We can't afford to worry about one or two naked bodies. But what we absolutely need to avoid right now is any chance that your true identity could be revealed."

"Huh?"

"We can talk about the details inside. We don't have a lot of time to spare, so let's keep any vulnerable moments to a minimum," Kuroe said, urging him to get started.

Still somewhat uncertain, Mushiki pulled out a clothes basket—only to stop midway.

"Kuroe?" he asked.

"What is it? Why do you look so serious all of a sudden?"

"If we're taking a bath...that means undressing, right?"

"...Well, yes."

"Of course, there's no way Saika's beautiful body could be lacking in any way. She's a supreme work of art. There shouldn't be any shame in showing it off, no? Besides, I'm a man, a high schooler at the peak of puberty. To be honest with you, I would kill to get a look at this body. I want to etch that sight into my very mind. And if I'm going to wash myself, naturally that means I'm going to be touching things that are normally out of reach. My heart's racing with excitement here."

"I think it would be best if you didn't speak such thoughts aloud," Kuroe said with a raised eyebrow.

Mushiki, however, ignored her, his voice feverish: "But, but...! Even if she's basically unconscious, Saika's body still belongs to her. I can't look at it, I can't touch it, I can't feel it up...not without her permission...!"

"Your behavior doesn't exactly add up, you realize?" Kuroe said, sounding disgusted. Nonetheless, she did eventually give him a small nod. "Given the circumstances, I'm sure Lady Saika will allow you to some extent... But I can't say I don't understand where you're coming from. I'm surprised. You're quite the gentleman inside."

"Thank you. Yep, I'd rather build up this relationship properly than take advantage of her in some underhanded way. Discretion is important."

"Are you trying to see how fast you can get me to retract my previous statement?" Kuroe paused before letting out a deep sigh as she retrieved what looked like a long piece of black cloth from her pocket. "But I understand. I will try to accommodate you as best I can."

"What's that?" Mushiki asked.

"Excuse me," Kuroe said in response before covering his eyes with the strip of cloth.

Mushiki was taken aback at being blindfolded all of a sudden, but it wasn't long before he understood Kuroe's intentions.

Right. This way, he wouldn't be able to steal a glimpse of Saika's naked body.

"Ah... But isn't it dangerous to take a bath blindfolded...? I mean, what if I slip and fall?"

"You needn't worry about that. We'll bathe together, and I'll take care of everything. Washing your hair, your body, changing you into your clothes."

"I think that's another problem, though..."

"There's no problem. I've served Lady Saika this way before."

"Huh...?! H-hold on, tell me more!"

"I doubt there will be any issue, but all the same, I'll have to strongly decline. Now, let me undress you."

Before he knew it, Kuroe had already reached out, her hands gliding over his body as she removed his uniform piece by piece.

"Kyargh... Th-that was a little fast..." He gasped at this unexpected feeling.

It was a new experience for him, being stripped naked by someone else. Moreover, being blindfolded, he couldn't know where her hands would go next. His heart raced as this unforeseen danger game began.

Kuroe showed no sign of slowing down or stopping.

Before he knew it, the moment of truth was upon him. He sensed her hand circling around his back, then he heard a soft click, and the band that had been wrapped tightly around his chest came undone.

"Whoa..."

Barely a second had passed since he realized that the bra had been unhooked. The two weights at his chest were so substantial that he almost reached out to support them with his hands.

"...Kuroe," he called out, trying to calm his ragged breathing.

"What?"

"Sure, I can't see them...but this still feels wrong."

"...Maybe I *should* have knocked you out?" Kuroe remarked, her cold tone suggesting that she may in fact have actually considered that option.

She grasped his neck in her hand, leaving Mushiki with the unmistakable impression that if he was to say any more, she might follow through on that threat and clamp down on his carotid artery, so he kept his response to an unsteady shake of his head.

Then, from in front of him, he made out a faint rustling sound.

Naturally, his eyebrows pulled up in suspicion.

"...Um, Kuroe? What was that?"

"I'm just getting ready. Don't mind me," she said as something soft pressed against his arm.

"Hyargh?!" he cried out, a tremor coursing through his body.

"Excuse me," Kuroe's cool voice sounded. "I'm pressing my body against yours to guide you into the bathing area."

"A-ah... R-right... I-I'm not imagining this, am I? Have you taken off your clothes, too?"

"Of course."

"...Why?"

"What an odd question. They would get wet otherwise."

That isn't the point, Mushiki felt like saying, but his throat clamped up.

Kuroe clung even more snugly to him than she had a moment ago.

"Hey, Kuroe? Um, aren't you a little close...?"

"You can't see at the moment. I can't allow you to trip and hurt yourself. Now, come this way."

Mushiki had no idea what on earth was going on anymore, so he allowed her to lead him into the bathing area and sit him down on a stool.

"Now then, I'm going to pour some warm water over your shoulders."

"O-okay..."

No sooner did he finish responding than she did just that. The temperature was perfect, neither too hot nor too cold.

After repeating this several times, she began to wash his hair with a practiced hand.

His hair hadn't been anywhere near this long in his original body, so it was an uncanny feeling.

"...Speaking of which, about that previous topic," said Kuroe as she washed his hair, having just remembered something.

"Previous topic...? You mean about me returning to my original body? Or that I shouldn't enter the girls' bathing area?"

"Both."

"What do you mean?"

She lathered his hair in foam and began to gently massage his scalp. "I've never seen another example of a merged human being, so I'm only speculating here, but I think the reason why your body transformed back into your original form had something to do with the amount of magical energy being released."

"Magical energy...? You mean, because it's leaking all over the place...?"

"Yes. The situation has yet to be brought under control, so Lady Saika's magic continued to be released from your body little by little." Kuroe stopped there, rinsed off the shampoo, and then began to carefully apply a treatment to his hair. "Lady Saika has an enormous reserve of magical energy, and there is certainly no chance of it being exhausted this way... However, when the amount being released increases past a certain level, there is a chance that the body will respond with a defensive reaction."

"A defensive reaction...?"

"To put it simply, I believe that when the body detects a serious abnormality, it automatically enters a state of low magical energy consumption. Effectively, a kind of safe mode."

"Ah..."

Underneath the blindfold, Mushiki blinked several times.

Right now, the body of the most powerful mage in the world had been combined with that of a complete amateur, resulting in this distorted state.

As such, if those elements that comprised Mushiki were to manifest more strongly, the natural result would be that the total amount of magical energy being consumed would decrease.

"I see... That's a good analogy, huh?" He sighed in understanding. "So when you made my body transform back into Saika's..."

"You mean the kiss?"

With Kuroe putting that so bluntly, Mushiki found himself momentarily at a loss for words. "Yeah. What was that?"

"I offered you more magical energy. That seemed like the most efficient solution," she said indifferently.

Maybe this all meant nothing to her? Mushiki felt somewhat embarrassed that he seemed to be the only one bothered by her behavior, so he tried to change the topic.

"...So it's all about the amount of magical energy being released? I guess I did let a lot out in the classroom earlier, and there was a bit of a close call during the practical class afterward... Ah, and there was that fight with Anviet yesterday, too. A guess it all just piled up, huh?"

"Well, they probably contributed to it, but I'm referring more to moments when you aren't using magic. I suspect the immediate trigger might have been something else entirely."

"Huh?" Mushiki's expression at this was one of genuine puzzlement.

But then, as though to wash that look from his face, Kuroe ran the shower over his head once more.

"One's state of mind has a considerable effect on the flow of one's magical energy and its total amount. Determination, anger, excitement— emotions like those can often grant a mage more power than they would otherwise possess."

"So what you're saying is...," Mushiki said hesitantly.

"When you were in the girls' locker room," Kuroe said dispassionately, "perhaps your *excitement*, so to speak, triggered an increase in the flow of your magical energy."

"...Ahem..."

Mushiki could let out only a pained moan. Kuroe's accusation had struck too close to home.

"Hey... Um, I mean, I didn't really...you know..."

"If you say so," Kuroe said.

Mushiki felt somewhat pathetic but continued on. "In other words, that sign in front of the bathing area...?"

"Yes. You wouldn't be able to last seeing other women in their underwear, let alone naked. If you *did* see anyone in such a state, you would be outed immediately."

"..." Mushiki, still overwhelmed by a sense of self-disgust, fell silent.

At that moment, Kuroe said something amusing: "You mentioned you fell in love with Lady Saika at first sight, didn't you? It's interesting, don't you think, how men are capable of being aroused by a woman irrespective of her age? Then again, maybe that's proof of a healthy physiology."

"Oh, I've got my heart set on her!"

"Is that so? I suppose I can rest at ease, then," Kuroe responded.

The next moment, without any warning, there came an audible plopping sound as something soft pressed against Mushiki's—or strictly speaking, Saika's—breast.

"Kyah!"

The sudden, furtive graze prompted him to let out a loud screech as he arched his back.

That mysterious touch paid him no mind as it crawled across his neck, his abdomen, his buttocks, and everywhere else across his body without even the faintest hint of restraint.

"K-Kuroe..."

"Is something the matter? I'm not Lady Saika, you realize?"

"No, n-n-no. That isn't what I—"

Mushiki stammered, doing his best to pull himself free from her roving hands.

Nonetheless, those hands knew no restraint as they traveled across his skin, and Mushiki soon found himself succumbing to their touch.

"O-ooohhh..."

"Hmm." Seeing his reaction, Kuroe let out a small growl. "Mushiki. We may have a problem here."

"Wh-what problem...?"

"You look just like Lady Saika, but you're too talkative, and your reactions are too innocent. I have to admit: I'm having a little too much fun here."

"What...?!" Mushiki cried out, but Kuroe's hands didn't stop what they were doing.

She continued to rub the sponge across his skin in every possible direction. "Now then, raise your arms. I'll leave your whole body shining."

"Hold on a min— K-kyaaarrrggghhh?!"

Mushiki's wailing voice echoed throughout the expansive bathing area.

"...?!"

All of a sudden, Ruri, lying on her bed in Room 314 of the first girls' dormitory building at Void's Garden, opened her eyes and sat up.

"Ah, you're awake. Are you okay...? Wh-what's wrong, Ruri?" asked Hizumi, who had been reading a book in her chair, her expression serious.

"...Did you hear something just now?"

"...What do you mean?"

"It was...almost like Madam Witch's voice, like she had just discovered a sensation she's never felt before...something halfway between shame and pleasure...I guess?"

As Ruri attempted to translate the vague information she had heard into meaning, Hizumi gave her a confused look. "Huh? I didn't hear anything... Are you sure it wasn't a dream?"

"Yeah. It was faint, but I definitely..." She cut off there before raising her face, as though having heard it again. "...?! Hold on. Did you hear it...?"

"Eh...? Madam Witch's voice?"

"I don't think so... It was lower this time... I can't believe it... It's like it's being violated by incessant pleasure... But that's not all... There's something almost nostalgic about it... It reminds me of my brother..." She forced her eyes shut as she attempted to convey those vague sensations.

Hizumi covered her mouth with her hand. "Ruri, do you miss your brother so much that you're hallucinating about him...?"

"Wh-what? No way...!"

"But didn't you say after our practical class that you thought you heard his voice somewhere...? But how could he even be in the Garden in the first place? It's a little strange, don't you think?"

"W-well, that's..." Ruri drew her brow together in a frown. "It *is* strange... There's no way I could mistake my own brother's voice..."

"Good morning, Mushiki."

"...Good morning, Kuroe," he responded when he awoke the following morning, his mind in a haze. "Um, I have a question."

"What is it?"

"Why are you lying on top of me?"

"So you don't escape," Kuroe answered flatly.

"Is there some reason why I would *want* to escape?" he asked apprehensively.

Yes, Mushiki was currently in his room in the girls' dormitory at Void's Garden. Lying in bed, in Saika's body.

The events of the previous day must have left him exhausted, as he had fallen asleep almost immediately, and yet...

When he woke up, there in front of him was Kuroe, even though she ought to have been in her room next to his.

She was lying directly on top of him, straddling his abdomen with her thighs as she stared down at Mushiki's face. If he wasn't mistaken, this position was known as the *mount*. If this had happened to him while in a fight, he would have been left helpless.

"Calm down, please," he cried out. "I don't know what ongoing feud you have with Saika, but violence isn't the answer."

"You seem to have misunderstood something."

"No matter how gorgeous Saika's looks, envy never did anyone any favors!"

"I suddenly feel like capitalizing on this position," Kuroe growled as she rolled her shoulders.

Mushiki let out a choked squeal. "I'm kidding. Now, let's get down to business, please?"

"*Get down to business?*" Kuroe repeated before giving him a small nod and lifting her hands.

Then, in one continuous movement, she began to untie the ribbon that she wore around her neck.

"...? Kuroe?" Mushiki asked uncertainly.

Without answering him, she undid the buttons on her clothes one by one.

She was practically undressing while sitting directly on top of him.

"What...what are you doing, Kuroe?!" he demanded, panicked.

"Don't look away," she answered, sounding indifferent as she continued to undo the fastenings. "Look closely."

It wasn't long before all those buttons were undone, and her clothes, until then fitting her perfectly, had become rather sloppy in appearance.

Next, she brought her hand to her neckline, exposing her left shoulder—and the gorgeous, fair skin that lay beneath her blouse.

"...?!"

At that moment, Mushiki found himself squeezing his eyes tightly shut.

"Oh. That isn't fair, Mushiki. Look at me."

"Get dressed, then!"

She tried to get him to look at her by pulling at his eyelids and tickling his neck, but when those attempts had little effect, she let out a small sigh. "I suppose you leave me with no choice. Let's switch to Plan B."

"...?! Kuroe?!"

Having forced his eyes shut, he couldn't actually see her, but it was clear that she was now leaning directly over him. His nose filled with the faint aroma of her scented shampoo.

Mushiki stiffened. What on earth was he supposed to do in this situation?! But before an answer could reveal itself, Kuroe caught him unawares, whispering softly into his ears. "Cupcakes are Lady Saika's favorite food."

"What...?!"

Kuroe's sweet breath. A whisper that tickled his eardrums. Then the shocking revelation.

The moment that his mind processed everything, Mushiki's heart contracted.

Her onslaught didn't end there. Stroking his ears with her fingers, she continued. "When she washes herself, she always begins with her butt cheeks."

"...!"

To top it all off, Kuroe then delivered the final blow. "Lady's Saika's bust-waist-hip measurements...are eighty-eight, fifty-nine, and eighty-six."

"...?!"

A sudden heat was building up inside him, his breathing becoming ragged. He felt a slight dizziness coming on, his eyes losing focus. Then his whole body began to emanate a light glow, and—

"...Huh?"

The exclamation came from the voice of a man.

Yes, at that moment, Mushiki's body had just transformed from Saika's back to his own.

"Hmm. It looks like my attempt to prompt a state conversion was successful," Kuroe said coolly as she pulled herself back up.

Mushiki scratched at his cheek in consternation. "Um, Kuroe, was that...?"

"Yes. I was trying to excite you to trigger a transformation... Although, I didn't expect it to happen so quickly," she said, still staring at her exposed left shoulder.

"..."

For some reason, Mushiki felt strangely embarrassed and self-conscious. But why? It wasn't like he had done it on purpose or that he had had any ulterior motives.

Nonetheless, he didn't fail to notice it. Kuroe, now fixing her clothes, let out a small sigh.

"...Is it me, or do you look relieved, Kuroe?"

"...Do I?" she answered sternly.

Mushiki watched on doubtfully.

Kuroe cleared her throat as she stood up from the bed and changed the topic. "But that isn't important. We don't have much time. You'll have to get ready before the other students wake up."

"Get ready...? For what?"

"Isn't it obvious?" she replied quizzically, as though the answer ought to have been a matter of course.

"And so, beginning today, we have two new additions to our class—Mushiki Kuga and Kuroe Karasuma."

A few hours after waking up in his dormitory room, Mushiki, now dressed in a boy's Garden uniform, found himself standing in the exact same place in the exact same classroom as the day before.

Though, not everything was the same as yesterday.

In appearance, he was no longer Saika Kuozaki but rather had returned to his own body. For that reason, his introduction was delivered with a different sense of urgency than the day before. The class gave curious stares, attempting to size him up.

"..."

No, that change wasn't the problem here.

Mushiki turned to the girl beside him (similarly dressed in a school uniform of her own) and whispered, "Kuroe?"

"What is it?"

"Um... Why did I have to transfer in as *me* this time? And you're joining the class, too?"

Still facing the room and standing with her back straight, Kuroe answered, "Considering what happened yesterday, there's no telling what might trigger another state conversion—or when."

"So I'm like a ticking time bomb or something?"

"That's an apt expression," Kuroe answered coolly. "If by chance someone was to spot you in your own body, Mushiki, it would pose a significant problem for us. This Garden is supposed to be hidden from the outside world. Any outsider who managed to slip in would be subjected to a thorough inquisition." She stopped briefly before continuing. "This way, if you are enrolled in the school as Mushiki Kuga, even if only nominally, we can reduce the severity of such a situation. You won't be an unidentified intruder who has somehow managed to infiltrate the campus, but rather a delinquent student skipping class... As for *my* being here, this will allow me to trigger another state conversion on short notice should it prove necessary."

"...Right." Mushiki nodded before realizing a fatal flaw in her plan. "But if something was to happen in the girls' locker room, like it almost did yesterday, everyone would think I did that."

"Well..."

"Well?"

"Try not to let that happen."

"Can you stop acting so nonchalant, please?" Mushiki whispered, worried that the two of them had been talking at the front of the room for too long.

The homeroom teacher, Tomoe Kurieda, looked toward them in apparent exasperation. "Mushiki? Karasuma? What are you both talking about? I'm not at all impressed. The two of you whispering in class on your very first day...," she said, crossing her arms.

"Ah, sor—" But before he could finish that apology, he stopped himself. "...? Ms. Kurieda, right?"

Tomoe's appearance should have been exactly the same as it had been the day before, but there was something different about her face, gestures, and voice.

Yesterday, she had worn a frightened expression, hunching over and curling up like a quivering Chihuahua.

Now, however, her bearing was one of confidence, her posture serving

Kuroe
Karasuma

Mushiki
Kuga

to emphasize her incredible proportions. Her graceful and leisurely demeanor called to mind the supple image of a female panther.

"Hmm...? Have we met before? Oh-ho, or are you trying a pickup line on me in front of the whole class?"

"Um, er, that isn't what I meant..." Mushiki shook his head in an attempt to defuse the situation.

Tomoe, however, licked her lips, narrowed her eyes, and stroked Mushiki's chin with the tip of her finger... "Oh-ho... That *is* a rather generic pickup strategy, but I don't mind. You've got some audacity. I'll play along. Come see me in the staff room after school. I'll give you one of my *special extracurricular lessons*," she said in a sexy whisper.

Mushiki's eyes all but popped from their sockets at this stark difference in her attitude.

At that moment, Kuroe glanced deliberately toward the door at the side of the room. "Oh! Good morning, Lady Saika."

"Kyaaarrrggghhh...?! N-n-no, it isn't what it looks like, Madam Witch...! It's all a misunderstanding! I would never, ever try to seduce a pretty young boy while on duty...!"

All of a sudden, Tomoe, who had until just then been emitting a sickly scent of self-confidence and seductive sex appeal, fell to the floor with tears in her eyes, pressing her forehead against the ground as though begging for her very life.

"Oops, excuse me. I must have mistaken someone else for her."

"U-ugh... Be more careful in the future, please. You made my heart skip a beat just then. You could have shaved years off my life span... Anyway, Kuga, see me after—"

"Ah. I think it might be Lady Saika, after all."

"Kyaaarrrggghhh! I'm kidding! You know I have a weak heart, Madam Witch! I would never say something like that seriously! It's just one of my little jokes... Ohhh! I'm sure I'll live an even longer life by worshipping you, Madam Witch...! Thank you, thank you!"

Once again, Tomoe was lying flat on the floor like an obsequious grasshopper.

Kuroe stared down at her coldly before glancing back at Mushiki. "Don't worry. Lady Saika will be absent today."

With that announcement, the other students, watching on with bated breaths, let out sighs of relief. They were probably all on tenterhooks, wondering when Saika would arrive to join them.

Tomoe was the only one who didn't seem to hear her, still bowing her head low to the ground.

"Well, the teacher doesn't look ready to get up yet. Let's take our seats," Kuroe suggested.

"...Right."

Following Kuroe's lead did seem to be the best way forward here, so Mushiki left Tomoe, still cowering on the floor at the prospect of Saika's reappearance, to the back of the room.

Only then did he notice it.

While most students were watching Tomoe's scandalous behavior with some combination of forced smiles and abject shock, one was staring straight at Mushiki, her face awash with pure astonishment.

"Wh-wh-what...?"

It was the genius mage, the knight serving directly under the school's headmistress, and Mushiki's younger sister, who had last seen him back when their parents separated.

With a rattling clatter, Ruri Fuyajoh rose to her feet and pointed at him.

"...What are *you* doing *here*, Mushiki...?!" she cried.

The suddenness of her outburst prompted the remaining students to turn her way in surprise, then to follow her outstretched hand until their eyes rested on Mushiki.

"Huh...? Do you know him?"

"Didn't we see him in the corridor this morning, though?"

As various voices echoed throughout the room, Hizumi's eyes opened wide in sudden remembrance. "I thought I recognized that name... Don't tell me; is he your brother, Ruri...?"

That exclamation only added fuel to the fire that had already engulfed the room.

"Eh? Didn't you say your brother was born in April?"

"But Ruri was born in March, so even though he's almost a year older than her, that would put them in the same year level."

"He's the one you gave a picture frame made of seashells to for his fifth birthday?"

"The one with the charming little mole on his neck?"

"Huh? How do all these people I've never even met before know so much about me?" Mushiki exclaimed, the sound of his voice adding to the chorus coming as a surprise even to himself.

Then, as though offering an answer to that question, all eyes turned to Ruri... Apparently, she was the source of that information.

"..."

Nonetheless, Ruri, seemingly unable to hear those around her, took one shaky step after another toward Mushiki.

Only then, fixing him in her fiery gaze, did she say: "I'll ask you again. What are you doing at the Garden? No...first of all, how did you even find out about this place? Were you scouted by the administrative department? Or did another Fuyajoh put this idea in your head?" Using an aggressive voice, she interrogated him.

Menace, power, resolution—there were many words for it, but she exuded an invisible sense of pressure that had been handed down across the generations, and at that moment, Mushiki was experiencing it firsthand. Perhaps his classmates had sensed it, too, as they remained completely silent.

The atmosphere in the room was indeed different from yesterday and the excitement when Saika had joined the class. It was as though some ancient instinct, lost amid the peace of modern civilization, had just been reawakened. It was a feeling of being confronted by an apex predator, a commanding force that would take no half answers.

At that moment, Ruri felt so *real* that even Mushiki, with all his ignorance and inexperience, could sense it.

"Ruri..."

Of course, he could hardly give her an honest answer with everyone watching. It would be a betrayal to Saika and could even put his own life in jeopardy.

It was clear that she wouldn't accept any lies, and something told him that she would see straight through any attempt at deception.

As such, he decided to lay bare his true feelings free from deceit and came out with the words he had been unable to give voice to in Saika's body: "I'm so happy to see you again, Ruri."

"Ngh?!" She spun around, letting out a crazed cry.

Her face had turned bright red, her eyes swimming like a pair of migratory fish.

Nevertheless, she soon regained her mental fortitude, straightening her back as she took in a deep breath. Perhaps she was sweating a little, as her bangs stuck to her forehead.

"...Y-you can't fool me. Give me a proper answer—"

"Look at you. You've grown into a real beauty, Ruri."

"Guew-eh-geh-heh...!" She choked, her appearance at that moment somewhat far from beautiful.

Mushiki rushed over, sitting her back down and patting her on the back. "Are you all right? There's no need to rush, so just—"

"...!"

A moment later, she suddenly jerked away, jumping up and fleeing from his outstretched hand.

Then, glaring at him, her face as red as a tomato and with tears streaming down her eyes, she cried, "D-don't think you've won! I won't accept this! I swear, I'm going to get you kicked out of this Garden! I swear it! Aaauuuggghhh!"

With that, she bolted for the entrance and disappeared into the hallway.

A pensive air filled the classroom, until finally the bell rang to signal the end of homeroom.

Around ten minutes later, once Tomoe Kurieda finally regained her composure, the first class of the day started.

"In other words, just because a new discovery has ushered in a new generation doesn't mean that old techniques are rendered meaningless. Rather..."

As with the day before, Tomoe was making use of the electronic blackboard as she continued her lecture on the history of magic.

No, actually, there *was* something different from the previous day, unflattering though it might be to point out. Unlike yesterday, when she had been visibly intimidated by Saika's presence, she now came across as truly imposing.

She had puffed out her chest with confidence, and her words were flowing one after the next without a hint of hesitation. She even had the presence of mind to joke with the students sometimes, inviting every now and then the occasional laugh. This, no doubt, was her usual teaching style.

The overall mood in the classroom was much more relaxed this time around.

Mushiki was naturally attracting some attention, but all the same, his classmates seemed considerably more at ease. That said, a few continued to watch his every move.

Well, there was *one* female student who kept glowering at him.

Yes, while Ruri had fled from the classroom, she returned to her seat in time for first period.

The siblings had managed to become the center of attention, but with Ruri's steely mental fortitude, she didn't seem to be particularly bothered by it.

"...Mushiki." Perhaps that stare was getting to *her*, though, as with Tomoe still lecturing at the front of the room, Kuroe whispered across to him.

"What now, Kuroe?"

"You did mention that you and Knight Fuyajoh are brother and sister, but was your relationship an acrimonious one, by any chance?"

"No, I wouldn't say that... We got along well."

"Then why is she glaring at you like that?"

"Well...," Mushiki murmured, at a loss for an answer.

At that moment, Tomoe, standing beside the teacher's table, pointed straight at him. "Kuga! I can see that you're excited about your first class, but no private conversations while I'm talking, okay?"

"Ah... Sorry."

"Hmm, you're a hopeless one, aren't you? Yep, you're going to need some discipline, I think. A firm hand. After school—"

"Look," Kuroe said, pointing into the hallway as though having just noticed something.

Tomoe fell silent, glancing nervously behind her. "Eh... It isn't *her*, is it?" Fear having taken hold of her, she glanced carefully through the entrance, inspected the corridor, then returned to her position by the electronic blackboard with a look of relief.

Then, after taking a deep breath to calm herself, she turned back to Mushiki. "Well, never mind. So, Kuga. If you have time to chat, that must mean you already understand what we're here to learn, no? Why don't you try answering a few questions, then?"

"Um, but I don't really understand...," he answered without delay.

Tomoe nonetheless let out a fearless laugh. "In that case, I wish you could at least *act* a little more worried for me, though..."

"Sorry," Mushiki said. "But I still don't really understand what magic actually is in the first place..."

With that admission, he heard the others throughout the room exhaling in exasperation or otherwise letting out amused chuckles.

The meaning behind those words was almost identical to what he had said the day before, but the reactions now were at stark odds to when Saika had asked a similar question.

"Come on, seriously? How did an amateur like this even get into our prestigious Garden?" said a tall male student with an exaggerated shrug (incidentally, the very same student who had described Saika's similar query as deep and profound).

"Oh dear... Does he really think he's on the same level as the rest of us?" A bespectacled female student added (the same one who had held her head in her hands in acute distress when he had asked about magic and magical energy).

"Heh… Look how dumb and naive he is. This'll be interesting," said a male student sitting by the window as he brushed a hand through his long bangs (he had praised Saika's question as thought-provoking and insightful).

And finally…

"…Ah?"

Perhaps in response to those other reactions, a chilling voice echoed throughout the room.

Ruri glanced around with bloodshot eyes, her brow wrinkled, veins throbbing on her forehead.

"…?!"

Pinned down by her gaze, the students who had been laughing at Mushiki's expense fell suddenly silent.

Nonetheless, Ruri herself said nothing more.

Having announced that she would throw him out of the Garden, she could hardly come to his defense now. That said, she wouldn't stand to hear anyone other than herself speak ill of him, either. Or so it seemed to Mushiki. She was almost like a rival character in a boys' comic book.

"R-Ruri? Ruri…?" Hizumi asked, flustered as she tapped her on the shoulder.

Finally, bringing her anger back under control, Ruri let out a loud snort and turned back to the front of the room.

"…Er, um… I-is it okay to continue the lesson…?" Tomoe, having no doubt sensed the fraught atmosphere, was visibly sweating.

"Of course," Ruri answered matter-of-factly. "Hurry along, please. This *is* your job, isn't it?"

"Uh…"

After that snide remark, pulling a long face, Tomoe reluctantly turned back to the class.

After somehow pulling through that distressing lecture, third period finally rolled around, and Mushiki headed to the training hall at the central school building with the rest of his class. Like fifth and sixth periods yesterday, it was time for another of Anviet's practical skills classes.

Having changed into his gym clothes, Mushiki shrugged lightly as he stepped foot into the hall.

Like his uniform, the outfit Kuroe had picked out for him fit perfectly. He had no idea when she had managed to take his measurements, but she was clearly very diligent.

"I was a little concerned about letting you out of my sight, but it looks like I needn't have worried," sounded a voice from behind him.

Mushiki glanced over his shoulder and laid eyes on Kuroe, dressed in the same style of gym clothes as him.

"Huh? But a state conversion from Saika's body to mine should only happen when I release too much magical energy, right?"

"I expect so, but this *is* the first time I've ever actually dealt with two people merged into one. You never know."

Mushiki could only force a smile at that off-putting remark. "Well... I'll be okay. I mean, I'm using the men's locker room this time. Seriously, it's wonderful. With no girls around, you really can relax in there."

"That statement could invite a misunderstanding," Kuroe said, watching him through narrowed eyes.

At that moment, Anviet came in from the back of the training hall. "All right, let's get started. Gather round, you hear?" he said as though weighed down, beckoning lazily.

As a group, the students lined up in front of him.

"Okay, then. Once you're finished with the prep exercises, we're gonna continue with the same practice we started yesterday. We've got a lot of targets, so we'll divide into groups, and..." His voice dropped off there.

For a second, Mushiki wondered whether something had gone wrong, but it wasn't long before he realized what exactly it was.

Among the students, Ruri was holding her hand raised high into the air.

"Can I ask something, Mr. Svarner?"

"Ngh. Fuyajoh? What do you want?"

"We have two new transfer students today. This will be their first practical class."

"Transfer students...? Ah, right, I did hear somethin' about that...," Anviet said as he rubbed the back of his head. He surveyed the assembled students before locking onto Mushiki and Kuroe. "You two... Huh? Aren't you Kuozaki's servant or somethin'? What are *you* doin' here?"

Kuroe paid his scowl little mind as she nodded back to him in greeting.

Looking like he had no interest in continuing that conversation, Anviet let out a loud snort and turned next to Mushiki. "And you are...?"

"Mushiki Kuga."

"Ah, right, got it. Let's see how memorable you are," Anviet said with a dismissive wave of his hand before turning back to Ruri. "There. Are you happy now? Newbies, if you don't know how to do the prep exercises, get one of these guys to teach you. As for the real trainin'...if you can handle it, good. If you can't, watch the others first. Observation is part of the learnin' process."

"Can I ask permission for something?" Ruri asked.

"Permission? What for?" Anviet responded suspiciously.

Ruri then turned her piercing gaze toward Mushiki. "To fight Mushiki Kuga in a mock battle."

"...Hah?"

"...!"

Anviet furrowed his brow at this challenge, while the other students watched in utter astonishment. Kuroe's eyes likewise twitched in concern.

Ruri's comment back in the classroom echoed in Mushiki's mind. She had said that she would throw him out of the Garden, though he wasn't sure why. Perhaps she meant to hurt him, to break his heart?

Had she chosen a mock battle in the middle of class over a duel or a sneak ambush out of a sense of discipline, or did she want her class-mates to witness the mortification from this unseemly encounter?

Whatever the case, the situation in the training hall took a turn for the worse.

Even so...

"...Huh? What're you goin' on about? There's no way I'm lettin' you fight in here," Anviet said sternly but decisively.

Ruri must have convinced herself that he would go along with her proposal, as her eyes showed dissatisfaction. "Why not?" she asked.

"*Why not...?* Maybe because you're an S-class mage, and he's a new-bie transfer student? You tell me, why *would* I allow it? Are you a battle maniac or somethin'...?"

"..."

Anviet's argument was a sound one, and Ruri could only bite her lip in frustration.

Somehow, Mushiki felt as if he could sense her bloodred gaze on him.

In truth, he felt a little sorry for her.

"Hey! Quit dawdlin' and get on those prep exercises! When you're done, run three laps around the trainin' ground and get your asses back here!" Anviet shouted, interrupting the frayed atmosphere that had fallen over the hall.

The students, though still looking ill at ease, did as instructed.

Ruri likewise started her preparatory exercises, though her eyes were bloodshot. If anything, she pushed herself more than anyone else in the room. When she ran, her arms and legs swung beautifully. She may have been his own sister, but Mushiki caught his breath in admiration at her diligence and dedication.

After finishing the warm-up exercises, the students gathered around once more in the center of the hall.

By then, Anviet had readied close to a dozen ball-shaped targets complete with arms and legs.

"One at a time, got that? Up to your second substantiations. If you can't handle them alone, you can surround the targets in groups of two or three. And if you slack off, I'll be there to give you a good kick in the ass!"

"*Right!*"

Following those orders, the students turned to their targets of choice, giving them their full attention.

"...!"

As he watched, Mushiki found himself rubbing his eyes in disbelief.

"Is something the matter, Mushiki?" Kuroe asked.

He blinked a few times before answering. "Ah, um... It's kind of vague, but I think I can see everyone's magical energy a little..."

Right. At this point in time, Mushiki wasn't in his Saika mode—and yet he could make out, albeit only vaguely, the magical energy emanating from his classmates' bodies.

Kuroe, however, didn't seem at all surprised as she nodded. "That isn't inconceivable. As I said before, the first hurdle to learning magic is being able to grasp a formerly unknown sense. But you, Mushiki, have already passed through that stage thanks to your merging with Lady Saika. Your mind is already that of a fully developed mage."

"What...?" He glanced down at his own hands. "Are you saying Saika has made my body mature, too?"

"In a manner of speaking," Kuroe said coolly before clearing her throat. "That being said, any other mage would be green with envy to have what you currently possess. After all, you have overcome the first hurdle unknowingly, all by drawing on the powers and abilities of the world's most powerful mage."

"...Does that mean I can actually *use* magic, then?"

"Something tells me it won't be that convenient... But you may at least be able to release some power. Why don't you give it a try?" With that, Kuroe pointed to a target on the far wall.

There, across the room, a small glowing ball complete with a pair of legs was standing there forlornly.

"Right. It might not work, but I'll give it a try."

Saying that, Mushiki faced his target and began to focus, doing his best to recall what it had felt like to wield magic in Saika's body.

"You, Munakata. You ain't channelin' your magical energy there properly. Don't think of your substantiations as weapons. Think of them as extensions of your limbs... And you, Mabuchi. If all you can pull off is your first substantiation, that'll do. You should still be able to get in a hit, so long as you focus. Find a way to get the result you want with the cards you have."

Anviet, his hands stuffed into his tracksuit pockets, was walking around the room giving each of the students advice in turn as they faced off against their targets.

One or two crests had appeared somewhere on each of the students' bodies, a telltale sign that they were activating their substantiation techniques.

It was a rare thing for a mage to be able to activate their second substantiation. *How many of these kids would be able to unlock their third substantiations over the course of their lifetimes?* Anviet wondered.

"...?!"

At that moment, as he surveyed the training hall, he felt a sudden chill run down his spine. He turned around.

It wasn't an exceptionally strong source of magical power that he had recognized, nor malevolent intent, but rather some sensation that he found difficult to put into words.

Nevertheless, his instincts as a mage, and his intuition as a knight, prevented him from regaining his composure.

"..."

Out of the corner of his eye, he spotted Ruri. She, it seemed, had noticed it, too, and was scanning the room intently.

What the hell?

Anviet gulped, his eyes opening wide.

Across the hall were several students, most of them struggling to reach their targets.

One was surrounded by a plume of wind, her first substantiation.

Another was wielding the massive hammer that characterized his second substantiation.

And another...one of the new transfer students, simply stood there, hands raised, no crest whatsoever appearing on his body.

"..."

At this last sight, Anviet found himself scratching at his cheek. "No way," he murmured, when—

"What...?!"

A loud alarm had begun to sound throughout the Garden, followed by countless cracks erupting in the sky overhead.

"Huh...?!"

Mushiki, his eyes squeezed shut from concentrating, suddenly glanced upward as the alarm echoed around them.

At that moment, several deep fissures broke through the sky hanging over the training hall.

"Mushiki," Kuroe called out, running toward him.

"Kuroe!" he called back, flustered. "Is this...?!"

That sound. This phenomenon.

It was just like what had happened the first day of his arrival at the Garden.

"There's no doubt about it. It's an annihilation factor. But to appear without warning like this..."

As though to silence her, one of the fissures hanging overhead tore larger and larger—until before they knew it, a huge, hulking monster began to emerge from behind it.

Razor-sharp claws. A body lined with toughened scales. Wings reminiscent of a bat. A head lined with horns and fangs.

Annihilation Factor No. 206: Dragon.

It was the exact same kind of mythical beast that Anviet had defeated with a single blow.

However, there was something decidedly different this time—the sheer number of those creatures.

Back then, there had been only one, though that alone had been enough to reduce the city beyond the Garden's walls into a sea of flames.

But now...

"A hundred...two hundred...no, there's more of them...?!" A lone, dismayed voice reverberated through the training hall.

Indeed. Those dragons were now so numerous, all but shrouding the sky above, that it was impossible to ascertain their exact number.

That wasn't all.

Deep amid the throng, through a massive spatial fissure, a giant specimen reared its head.

As he took in that sight, Anviet stared back wide-eyed. "Hah?! Annihilation Factor No. 48: Fafnir?! What the hell is a double-digit monster doing *here*?! And with all these dragons?!"

"This is no time for your whining! Get the students out of here!" Ruri thundered.

Her voice now was no longer that of a student, but of a knight, one of the Garden's most capable guardians.

"Like I need *you* to tell *me* that! B-class mages and above, return fire! C-class and below, fall back to the central area!"

"*R-right...!*"

As instructed, most of the students hurried to evacuate the training ground, with only a small few remaining behind.

As though having anticipated the students' attempt to flee to safety, several dragons descended from above, planting themselves directly in their path.

"Wh-whoa!"

"Kyah?!"

The students cowered in terror as the dragons let out tremendous roars.

"Tch..."

But before the creatures could attack those who had attempted to flee, two halo rings shimmered to life on Anviet's back.

"Second Substantiation: Vajdola!"

Two vajras appeared by his side as he fired a barrage of thunderbolts.

At that moment, the first dragon's head as it closed in on the students was dismembered and sent flying. With a heavy crash, its hulking body sank to the floor, disappearing in a burst of light.

"Are you okay?!"

"Y-yes!"

"Then get the hell out of here!" Anviet roared.

The students, though panicked, took off once more.

There was no end to the number of dragons. One after another, they descended onto the training ground, clearly unwilling to let even a single person escape.

"Ugh..." Frowning, Anviet used another lightning bolt to send a dragon's head flying, before shredding its wings and punching a huge hole through its body.

Mushiki was reminded of a thunder-clad god of war as he watched Anviet rage.

There was an obvious difference in their respective power levels. One after the next, he crushed dragon after dragon underfoot.

The problem, however, was the overwhelming number of those annihilation factors. Searching for gaps in Anviet's defenses, the dragons continued to charge toward the students.

Mushiki and Kuroe were no exception.

"Whoa...?!"

"...! Ngh..."

Seeing the two, a huge dragon descended from the sky. Kuroe threw herself in front of him, as though to use herself as a shield.

"Kuroe!" Mushiki cried, grabbing her by the shoulder and pulling her toward himself as he turned his back to the creature.

"Mushiki...?!" Her voice, tinged with astonishment, echoed in his ears.

The impact he was expecting failed to reach him.

"Second Substantiation: Luminous Blade!"

Just as Ruri's voice sounded out, the dragon's massive body was sliced into pieces before it could touch him or the other students.

"Wha—?"

With dismembered pieces of the dragon still raining around her, Ruri landed directly in front of him.

Two patterns reminiscent of demon masks had appeared above her head, while in her hands she grasped a *naginata*, its blade gleaming like a demonic will-o'-the-wisp.

For a moment, Mushiki caught his breath at the divine majesty of that sight.

Ruri, however, wore a grim expression as she grabbed him by the front of his shirt. "This is a mage's battlefield. I don't know how you found out about the Garden, but give it up! You're no mage...! Get out of here! And don't ever get involved in our world again!" she ordered him.

Then, in a quiet voice, she addressed Kuroe. "And you, Kuroe, was it? I don't know what interest an attendant to Madam Witch might have with Mushiki, but you must know how to handle yourself, right? Look after him for me."

With that, she took off, leaving a trail of light as she stormed toward the remaining dragons.

"...Mushiki."

As he watched on in dismay as Ruri fought up above, Kuroe, her arms crossed, called out to him in a disgruntled voice.

Flustered, Mushiki released her from his arms.

Kuroe's grim expression remained unchanged. Her brow still furrowed, she began to list her grievances. "What on earth were you thinking just then? How many times have I told you? Your body is Lady Saika's body. *Your* death would mean *her* death."

"Sorry. It just kind of happened."

"No, it didn't." Kuroe turned away, pouting. She looked legitimately angry this time.

Concerned, Mushiki glanced up once more. "B-but it worked out okay, huh? Anviet is here... And Ruri is pretty strong, too. Those dragons took me by surprise, but things are looking—"

"..." Though Mushiki had tried to make light of the situation, Kuroe wore a troubled look. "I wonder if it really will be that easy..."

"Huh?"

"The two of them are indeed a force to be reckoned with. Moreover, backup should be on the way soon. Eventually, they will be able to defeat all these annihilation factors... But there are so many of them. It's all but inevitable that they'll cause considerable damage."

"But once they're defeated, won't that undo all the destruction...?" Mushiki asked, remembering what had happened a few days prior.

Kuroe wrinkled her brow. "It's true—if the annihilation factors are defeated during the window for reversible destruction, this whole incident will be as if it never happened."

"Right. In that case—"

"However, that doesn't apply to those who have witnessed the annihilation factors themselves—mages, in other words."

"...! Are you saying if any mages die, that it will be permanent?" Mushiki demanded.

"That is *exactly* what I mean," Kuroe confirmed with a pained look. "There's only one person who could overcome this situation without suffering any casualties... Only one person who could eradicate all these dragons from the sky above us while sparing the mages down below."

Mushiki clenched his fists and muttered, "I can only think of one mage like that..."

"Aaauuuggghhh!"

With an ear-splitting cry, Ruri brought her *naginata* swinging down.

Her second substantiation, Luminous Blade. That sharp blade of light jutting out at the end of the weapon's long handle stretched like a whip, tracing an inexhaustible path as it lashed out at the annihilation factors emerging from all directions.

Not even those dragons with their tough hides and their all-consuming fiery breath posed much of a challenge for a Knight of the Garden. In fact, Ruri and Anviet had already defeated more than thirty of the creatures between them.

The problem, however, was their sheer number.

Countless dragons were still soaring above, attacking the Garden—and the outside world beyond its walls—one after the next. Through their collective efforts, the mages had somehow managed to pull through with minimal damage so far, but the surrounding city had already been reduced to smoldering ruins.

That horrendous sight could be restored so long as the annihilation factors were destroyed within the window for reversible destruction, but it was still a painful scene to see. Her brow furrowed in a deep frown, Ruri tightened her grip on her *naginata*.

Then, as though aiming for just that moment, a dragon lashed out with a plume of flames at the training ground, the air erupting with blistering heat.

"Tch..."

Ruri launched into the air, using her weapon to decapitate the fire-breathing monster. Even after its enormous head crashed into the ground, flames continued to scatter around it for a few seconds.

There were still several students lingering in the training hall, but they were keeping their distance from the other mages, and each seemed to be protecting themselves in their own way. As she evaluated the situation out of the corner of her eye, Ruri breathed a sigh of relief.

Then she noticed something.

Mushiki and Kuroe were nowhere to be seen.

"Mushiki...," she gasped, turning her gaze downward.

If he had managed to escape unharmed, that would be for the best. But her brother was an amateur, a newcomer fresh to the Garden. If he had been exposed to that sea of flames...

The most horrendous vision imaginable flashed before her eyes.

It only lasted for a brief moment, but in the heat of the battlefield, that was time enough to offer her foes a fatal opening.

"Gwah...?!"

By the time she saw it coming, the massive Fafnir-type annihilation factor had emerged from a long spatial fissure, the tall palisades of its fang-lined jaw opening wide.

She wouldn't be able to escape it. She clenched her teeth as she readied herself for the impact. She would have to manage, somehow, to withstand the blow so she could launch her own counterattack.

However—

"...Huh?"

The next moment, she found her eyes opening wide in shock.

The shot of pain she had been anticipating never came.

In its place, a tremendous sense of discomfort enveloped her entire body.

Indeed. Until just a short moment ago, her surroundings had been the training hall, the Garden, and a city reduced to a sea of flames.

Though what she saw laid out in front of her now...

...was a realm of frigid ice, with a powerful blizzard blowing all around.

"What...? This can't be..."

It was no joke or metaphor.

It was as if she had been transported in the blink of an eye, moved instantaneously from one place to another. If she were anyone else, she might have considered it a dream or an illusion.

However, Ruri was familiar with this phenomenon, this eerie sensation.

The supreme *domain* that transcends *phenomena*, that ultimately comprised *matter* through *assimilation*.

A fourth substantiation.

The ultimate form of magic, capable of forging a whole miniature world.

There was only one person who could pull off a feat of this magnitude...

"What a rude guest to attempt to wreak havoc in my Garden while I'm away."

"...!"

Ruri glanced up at the sound of that voice, calling out as though in response to her unspoken thoughts.

Then, as she took in the sight of the girl floating before her, her voice trembled. "Madam Witch..."

Indeed.

There, floating calmly before her with four whole crests activated above her head was the Witch of Resplendent Color, Saika Kuozaki.

For some reason, she was dressed in what looked like gym clothes—but Ruri was too shaken by emotion to think on it anymore.

Saika, aglow with the light of her crests, was staring down at the annihilation factors as they swarmed below.

"Kiss my feet... I will make all of you my brides," she said, slowly raising one hand into the air.

As she did, the storm raging around her began to pick up strength, a whirlwind building with her at its center.

"I-is that...?!"

"A tornado...?!"

The students were crying out in alarm below.

As though in response to their voices, a massive tornado swirling with piercing shards of ice struck the dragons all at once, centering around the Fafnir-type annihilation factor.

The hulking monsters were crushed beneath those icy fragments or else frozen by the subzero temperatures of the storm. Endless cries echoed through the sky but were soon drowned out by the blast of the icy tempest.

"Wh-whoooaaa?!"

"Kyaaarrrggghhh!"

Of course, it wasn't only the annihilation factors crying out, but the students, too.

Nonetheless—

"...!"

The next moment, Ruri blinked her eyes once more.

Just when she thought that the icy storm had engulfed her vision, the scenery around her changed all over again.

Yes, it was the same training ground where she and the others had been fighting just a moment earlier.

But now there wasn't a single dragon left to be seen—not even one.

The students were all safe and sound, though some were lying on their backs, their eyes unseeing, probably having fainted. Others crouched low, trembling in shock.

The whole incident couldn't have lasted more than a minute.

It truly was a miraculous outcome.

"Hmm... Sorry for causing a scene," Saika said playfully as she alighted on the ground.

No sooner did everyone realize what had happened than they erupted in cheers.

"..."

Touching her lips with her fingertips, Kuroe was wandering slowly across the training ground.

There was no longer any sign of the annihilation factors.

Mushiki, transformed into Lady Saika, had wiped them out with her fourth substantiation.

While it looked like he still couldn't exert proper control over his magic, it did seem that he was fully capable of wielding her powers without a problem. He was an unusual type of mage, that was certain.

Even so, from what Kuroe could tell, the students seemed to be unharmed. She couldn't find fault in the outcome.

"...Hmm."

Still...

She glanced overhead, her expression pained.

"Was that really a natural occurrence, so many annihilation factors emerging all at once...?"

Her doubtful murmur was soon drowned out by the cheers of the students behind her.

Chapter 4
⇌ Secret Rendezvous ⇌

Following the mysterious mass outbreak of annihilation factors, Mushiki, as Saika, paid a visit to the medical facilities in the Garden's eastern precinct.

The Garden's medical building was a large five-storied building, though in truth, it wasn't much different than a major hospital. The students who had been in the training hall during the attack were now gathered on the first floor.

That said, at first glance, none seemed to be badly injured. Even the worst among them had sustained nothing more than scratches or bruises. Rather than urgent medical treatment, the most prudent course of action was to give them all checkups as a precaution.

"Oh, Saika. That was a total disaster, no?"

Interrupting Mushiki's thoughts, a young girl clothed in a large white coat with a light underwear-like outfit underneath approached him from the back of the building.

It was Erulka Flaera, a mainstay of the Garden's knights. Incidentally, Mushiki remembered hearing that her usual role was overseeing the Garden's medical department.

"Ah, Erulka."

As Mushiki turned around, the students watching stood up straight in awe. Erulka, no doubt noticing their heightened attention, waved, the sleeves of her lab coat flapping delicately. "All right, all right," she said. "Don't overdo it if you're injured."

She glanced around, stroking her chin. "Hmm. Looks like we have a lot of patients. Which of you should we start with, I wonder...?"

With that, she brought her fingers together to make a special sign— and two red tattoo-like patterns appeared on her skin.

"Second Substantiation: Horkew."

No sooner did Erulka murmur those words than several creatures appeared around her—wolves complete with glowing fur and emblazoned with patterns similar to Erulka's crest.

There must have been more than a dozen of them in total, and they wasted no time responding to their summoner's gestured instructions and approaching the students gathered in the center of the room.

Sniffing their targets over, they began to lick the scratches and grazes that covered the students' bodies.

"Eh? Wh-what?"

"Bah! Ha-ha...!"

More than a few of the students contorted themselves in laughter at this tickling form of treatment.

"Keep quiet for a moment," Erulka cautioned the wolves, and with that, their tongues took on a faint glow, the wounds that they were seeing to slowly fading away.

"..."

Mushiki stared wide-eyed. He had heard about this technique from Kuroe, but even with that knowledge, he couldn't contain his amazement witnessing it with his own eyes.

"Hmm. I think we can leave this to my wolves here. This way, Saika. I know you wouldn't let an annihilation factor of that level harm you in any way, but just in case..."

"Huh?"

"The students are one thing, but we can't leave a mage of your caliber to my wolves, now, can we?"

"Ah. Oh." With that exclamation, Mushiki let Erulka lead him to an examination room at the end of the floor.

It was a small room, equipped with a desk, a cot, and two chairs. Erulka sat Mushiki down on the chair, then took a seat in the one across from him.

"Now, then." With a practiced motion, she grabbed the hem of Mushiki's gym top and pulled it up, exposing his abdomen and more to the open air.

"...?!"

He was doing his best to act as Saika would, but he couldn't stop his eyes from opening wide in surprise at her sudden action.

Erulka broke into a puzzled frown.

For a moment, Mushiki was gripped by a fear that he had failed to properly maintain character, but he soon realized he was mistaken. Rather, Erulka's gaze was fixed on his—or strictly speaking, Saika's—voluptuous breasts, poking out now that she had lifted his gym top.

"Hmm? Why aren't you wearing a bra?"

"Ah." Mushiki let out a soft gasp.

He was wearing proper women's sportswear, but that wasn't because he had changed clothes after transforming into Saika. As much as he would have liked to keep his true identity hidden, he simply hadn't had time to change.

According to Kuroe, clothes made from spirit thread, such as the school's uniforms and gym outfits, were enchanted to change shape to match the contours of their wearer—in this case, they had adjusted themselves when he had morphed from boy to girl.

However, this only meant that a men's shirt would become a women's one, that a pair of shirts and gym shorts would become more fitting. It didn't mean that new articles of clothing would appear where they hadn't been before.

Yes. In short, Mushiki, having transformed into Saika without having had time to prepare, was presently in a state of being braless.

"Ah, no, about that..." His eyes swam around in circles as he tried to conjure up some explanation that might be fitting of Saika's personality.

Though no matter how hard he thought, all he could come up with were sloppy excuses, careless reasons, or perverse oversights. Not one of them seemed plausible coming from Saika.

He was at a complete loss when Erulka's lips twisted in a grin.

"Well, they *are* a hassle, aren't they? I understand. If not for that Ruri, I wouldn't be wearing anything under my lab coat, either."

"...Ah-ha..."

Mushiki felt as if he had just been the subject of an uncomfortable misunderstanding, but he couldn't afford to protest now, so he offered only a vague smile.

It wasn't long before that smile gave way to startlement all over again.

Reason being—Erulka...was licking his belly.

"Hyargh...?!"

Before he knew it, he had let out a high-pitched squeal, pulling away.

Erulka stared up at him in wonder. "What was with that strange voice just now?"

"Ah, um... Erulka, what are you...?"

"Odd. A medical examination, of course. Sweat tells me a lot more than just words," Erulka said, fixing him with a strange look. "Saika... Are you feeling well...?"

"Huh? Wh-why do you ask?"

"Hmm. You just taste a little different than usual."

"...!"

Mushiki's heart seemed to skip a beat

Had Erulka realized he wasn't, in fact, entirely Saika...?

"Hmm...? Let me try again..."

"H-hold on a—"

With a smack of her lips, Erulka tried once more to stick her head beneath Mushiki's top, leaving him to push her head away in a panic.

He had no desire to continue this *medical examination*, as she put it, and have his true identity be revealed—and more importantly, his heart was still racing from when she had last licked him. If he wasn't careful, he could end up turning back into his own body directly in front of her.

"What are you doing? Do behave yourself, now."

"No, I'm okay, really, so..."

As the two of them engaged in a quiet game of cat and mouse inside the cramped examination room, there came an unexpected knock at the door.

"I'm sorry to disturb you, Ms. Erulka, but can I have a moment of your time?"

The next moment, a woman—a nurse, judging by her appearance—opened the door slightly.

Glancing up, Erulka arched an eyebrow in suspicion before quickly rising to her feet.

"Hmm. I'll be back in a moment. Stay right here," she said, pointing toward Mushiki as she left the room.

After watching her step outside, Mushiki breathed a sigh of relief. "That was...a close one...?"

The next moment, his body let out a faint glow, and he underwent another state conversion, shifting from his Saika mode back to his Mushiki mode.

Erulka really had been called outside in the nick of time. If not for that nurse's intervention, he may very well have transformed just as Erulka's tongue roved across his skin.

Nonetheless, he still couldn't let down his guard. As much as he hated leaving her high and dry, he would have to make a run for it before she came back.

Just as he reached out to open the door—

"Sorry to keep you waiting, Saika."

"Ugh."

After what seemed like only the briefest of interruptions, the door swung open, and Erulka stepped back inside.

Mushiki leaped backward in shock.

"Hmm?" Erulka glanced curiously around for a moment before stepping outside again to double-check the room number.

Finally, she directed her gaze to Mushiki. "Who are *you*? Where did Saika go?"

"Oh, um, well, she said something about having some urgent business to see to, so she left early. I was just walking by, so she asked me to let you know..."

Erulka let out a sigh, almost as though suspecting he was trying to pull one over on her. "I told her to *wait*. It's always the same with that one..."

Mushiki had thought it a rather pitiful excuse, but it looked like Erulka had bought it. He let out a relieved exhale and dipped his head. "In that case, I'll—"

"Hmm? Ah..."

Just as he was about to slip past her, Erulka's eyebrows twitched. "Hold on a second."

"...! W-was there anything else?" Mushiki stammered, his legs weighing him down as they stopped moving.

Suspicious, Erulka sniffed the air. "Have we met before?"

"I—I don't think so. Why do you ask?"

"There's something familiar about your scent..." She fell silent, pondering for a moment, before pointing back to the chair. "Sit."

"Huh?"

"I said *sit*. You're one of the students from the training hall, no? I'm free right now. I'll give you a special examination."

"Huh? M-me?"

"Just sit down already. Quickly now."

"...Right."

He would only serve to draw further attention to himself by refusing her any more than he already had, so resigning himself to his fate, Mushiki sat down in the chair.

Then, with a slight warmth rising in his cheeks, he began to roll up his gym shirt... He would have been lying if he had said he wasn't embarrassed, but at least he was unlikely to undergo another state conversion from his Mushiki mode back to his Saika one, so he would probably be okay.

Having affirmed his resolve, he waited—when Erulka stared back at him blankly.

"What are you doing?"

"...Huh? I thought you licked your patient's stomach when you examined them?"

Erulka's eyes opened wide at this remark, and she guffawed. "Ha-ha-ha, don't tell me you heard that from Saika? That's just for her."

"...Ah. Right..."

He had acted too hastily. Feeling even more embarrassed, he reluctantly lowered his rolled-up gym shirt.

At that moment, Erulka grabbed him by the hand. "And yet...even if Saika did tell you, it takes a certain amount of courage to roll up your shirt like that and expose yourself to a stranger. I wouldn't have expected such confidence from one with a face like yours... Very well. Perhaps this is fate, of a sort? Just for you, I'll give you a special lick."

"Huh? Uh... Eh?!" Mushiki cried out.

In a manner that didn't at all suit her petite frame and youthful appearance, Erulka gave him a lewd smile. "Now, then... Where should we begin?"

"Ugh, um, hold on a—"

Resistance is futile, she all but declared as she licked his abdomen. Mushiki let out a startled shriek.

At that moment, Erulka's eyebrows shot up in suspicion.

"...Hmm? This taste..."

"...!" Mushiki caught his breath.

Erulka, having licked his sweat while he was in Mushiki mode, seemed ill at ease. Could she have realized something?

"Hmm...? Perhaps it's just my imagination. Let me take another—"

"S-sorry, I really have to go...!"

"Stop! Wait!"

As Mushiki rushed to leave the examination room, Erulka reached out to grab him by his gym clothes.

"I-I'm fine! I'm completely uninjured!"

"I don't care! Just let me lick you! Come on, take off your clothes!"

"Aaahhh! Nooo!"

"Come on, it will all be over soon! Just lie down and count the stains on the ceiling!"

Once again, a fresh cat-and-mouse game, a new rough-and-tumble had erupted in the examination room.

Beyond the door, the other students in the waiting room could easily make out the pair's raised voices.

Afterward, rumors that Knight Erulka Flaera had been trying to get physical with a male student spread like wildfire, but at this moment in time, Mushiki was in no state to worry about such things.

"I've been looking all over for you, Mushiki. Where on earth have you been?"

About ten minutes after the attack in the examination room, Kuroe called out to Mushiki as he staggered down the corridors of the medical building.

"...And what made you transform again in such a short period of time? And why do your gym clothes look so worn-out? I take my eyes off you for a couple of minutes... Just what did you get up to? Something dirty, I'm sure..." Kuroe stared at him, her eyes filled with disdain.

Mushiki shook his head. "No, you've got the wrong idea, Kuroe."

After he explained the situation to her, Kuroe watched him through half-open eyes. "I see. Knight Erulka, you said? She hasn't learned your true identity, I hope?"

"No. It was a close call, but I don't think she caught on..."

Kuroe breathed a sigh of relief.

That respite was short-lived, though. Her expression quickly turned grim. "Mushiki. We need to talk. But there are too many people here. Please come with me."

"Huh? Ah, okay." He followed her down the medical building corridors.

Eventually, they arrived at a deserted area. Kuroe glanced around to make sure they were alone before speaking. "We will have to wait for the investigation department's report to know the details, but it appears that today's mass outbreak of annihilation factors may have been man-made."

"What...?" Mushiki's eyes shot open. "Are you saying those dragons attacked us on someone's orders?"

"I wouldn't go so far as to say that someone was *directly* using them. However, it's possible that the timing and location of the annihilation factors were somehow manipulated—or that a great number of annihilation factors were transferred to a single location."

"But how...? And aren't annihilation factors capable of destroying the whole world? Who would...?" But before Mushiki could finish that sentence, he suddenly fell silent.

No doubt having realized the same thing that he had, Kuroe gave him a brief nod. "Yes. A trick like that couldn't be pulled off by any ordinary mage. However..."

It was exactly as she said.

The same mage who had attacked both Saika and Mushiki could very well have been behind this latest incident.

"If you stop to think about it, it was exquisitely put together. A swarm of annihilation factors each of a level that they could easily be defeated individually. However, by the time they were all dealt with, there was a very real possibility that the students would be put in harm's way..."

"...So what you're saying is...," Mushiki began solemnly.

Kuroe nodded. "It was beautifully staged to confirm whether the Lady Saika currently present at the Garden is the real thing—to see whether *you* were capable of using her fourth substantiation."

"...So I'm...?" Mushiki fell silent, looking upset.

Kuroe, her eyes downcast, shook her head. "There is no need for you to feel responsible, Mushiki. If you hadn't acted, the students could have been injured. No doubt if Lady Saika was here, she would have done exactly the same thing. No, you should be proud, I think, that you successfully pulled off her fourth substantiation on such short notice."

"I know, right? This really is Saika's body, huh?"

"But it *is* strange. When you talk honestly, it makes me think that you *do* care a little." Kuroe sighed.

As she watched him through half-open eyes, Mushiki folded his arms in thought. "But this is bad, isn't it? If that really was caused by whoever attacked Saika and me..."

"Yes. They would have been able to confirm that Lady Saika is still alive. That said, we wouldn't have been able to keep that a secret forever. The truth would have come out sooner or later. Although..." Kuroe paused for a moment. "There is a certain course of action only available to us now that we know the assailant is aware of Lady Saika's survival."

"A certain course of action...?" Mushiki repeated.

"Yes," Kuroe answered before briefly explaining what she had in mind.

"...I see. But wouldn't that be pretty dangerous?" he asked.

"I won't deny it. But if we succeed, we should be able to fully identify your attacker or attackers. It's worth a try." With that, Kuroe spun around with a click of her heels. "I will examine any lingering traces left behind in the training hall. You, Mushiki, should return to your classes. In your present *excited* state, I doubt you will undergo another state conversion anytime soon."

"Um, Kuroe...?" Mushiki called out, but she had already disappeared down the corridor without looking back.

"..."

Left to himself, Mushiki stood there in stunned silence for a moment. After deciding that it would do him no good to remain that way forever, he started toward the medical treatment area, when—

"Mushikiii!"

"Huh?!"

No sooner did he step out from the room than a figure leaped out in front of him, the surprise sending him falling flat on his butt.

"Owww... Wh-what?" Mushiki frowned.

The girl now sitting astride him—Ruri—breathed an audible sigh of relief. "Mushiki! Ah, thank goodness you're okay...!"

She was out of breath as though having run all the way there, her sportswear damp with sweat. Judging by the redness around her eyes, it looked like she had been crying.

"Ruri...?"

"Don't scare me like that! When I lost sight of you, I—"

She stopped there, no doubt realizing that she and Mushiki were attracting considerable attention from the students and medical staff around them.

"...Come over here for a minute," she said brusquely, rising to her feet and tugging at his hand.

She led him out of the medical building, only releasing him once they had circled around to the back.

"I'm amazed you survived all that. I really thought you were dead," she said sullenly, folding her arms.

Mushiki's eyes opened wide. "Huh? You're acting different, aren't you? You seemed so worried..."

"What are you talking about? I wasn't *worried*..." Ruri played dumb, before her gaze sharpened. "Anyway, do you get it now? How dangerous it is to be a mage here at the Garden? I don't know how you found out about this place, but you're just not up to it. So pack your bags and get out of here. Forget everything you've seen here and go and live your life in peace," she ordered, pointing her finger right under his nose.

It *was* a sensible suggestion, but Mushiki found himself letting out a groan. "I'm sorry, Ruri. I know I'm not good enough. But I can't leave. I've got my own reasons."

"*Reasons...?* What *reasons?*" she demanded, squinting back at him.

Of course, he couldn't tell her the truth.

So he gave more pretext.

"Well... I've kind of...fallen in love with someone."

"Huh?" Ruri stared back at him blankly for a moment before—

"Whaaaaaaaaaaaaaaaaaaaat?!"

Her scream was so loud it could probably be heard from up in the heavens.

"Wh-wh-what the heck?! Y-you mean there's someone here, at the Garden, who you *like*?! You decided to become a mage just to get close to them?!"

"Um, yeah. The details are a little different, but that's basically it..."

"Ngh...?!" Ruri's eyebrows seemed to shoot halfway up her forehead, her eyes spinning in their sockets. "Th-that's...insane! Are you that stupid?! You threw yourself onto a real-life battlefield for something like *that*...?!"

"Sorry. But right now, nothing matters to me more."

"..." Ruri bit her lip in frustration at this last remark.

Almost as though she wanted to say something more.

She seemed to have second thoughts but ended up shaking her head. "N-nope, I can't accept it. That's just so, so..."

Looking conflicted, she seemed ready to say more—but having remembered something important, Mushiki interrupted her before she could continue.

"Right, Ruri. There's something I need to ask you."

"...Wh-what?" she demanded with a quizzical frown.

"I'm heading outside the Garden on Saturday, so if you're free, do you mind tagging along?"

"...Eh?" She stared back at him blankly for a while.

As her brain finally registered the meaning of his words, her eyes rounded in shock. "Wh-wh-what's *that* supposed to mean, all of a sudden?! Why would I—?"

"So it's no good? I really do need your help, though," Mushiki added.

"Ngh...?!"

In what seemed like less than a second, her face turned bright red. "D-don't tell me... This person you're chasing after; you don't mean—"

Then mumbling something under her breath, she turned her body away from him.

"Ruri?"

"...I-I'll think about it...! I'm thinking...!" she shouted as she wagged a finger under his chin before taking off down the pathway at a run.

"Hizumiii!" Ruri cried out at the top of her lungs as she slammed open the door to her dormitory room after classes.

Hizumi, who had returned to their room ahead of her, glanced timidly over her shoulder. "Huh?! Wh-what...?! Ah, Ruri? Good work tidying up after the attack. What's wrong?"

"It's an e-e-emergency! M-my brother!"

"Your brother...? You mean Kuga?"

"Right! That brother! H-h-he asked me out on a *date*!"

"A date...? But you're siblings? Don't you mean just talking together...?"

"No! He practically said it! *I came to this Garden because I love you, Ruri!*"

"Eh...eh?!" Hizumi exclaimed with alarm. "B-b-but...you're brother and sister... What...? Wh-what exactly did he say...?"

"He looked me right in the eye. And then he said: *I need you, Ruri*. And he had me cornered against a wall, I think...? Right... He was basically leaning over me all romantically... A-and then he lifted my face by my chin!"

Her interest piqued, Hizumi leaned forward, her cheeks having turned faintly pink. "W-wow... Despite his looks, Kuga sounds really up-front and assertive..."

"Wh-what am I supposed to do?! I've never been on a date before...!"

"Why are you asking *me* of all people...? Well, um, just so we're clear, you *are* thinking of going, right?"

"Of course! Why do you ask? I mean, my own brother invited me! I *have* to go!"

"No, I just mean... It sounds like he was hitting on you, is all."

"I get that... It's complicated, you know?! But that's that, and this is this!"

"R-right..." Hizumi scratched nervously at her reddened cheeks before asking: "Um... So when is it?"

"Saturday!"

"Saturday... A day off school, then. Well, you can't wear your uniform. First of all, you'll have to pick out something nice to wear, I suppose...?"

"That's it! Smart thinking, Hizumi! You know your stuff!"

"I wouldn't go that far..." Something about Hizumi's expression suggested she didn't totally agree with that assessment, but Ruri ignored her as she threw open the closet doors and began to sift carefully through the underwear folded up inside.

"The basics first. The top and bottom have to match... Maybe blue, like what I usually go with? Or maybe I should be a little more daring and try black...? Or I could use the garters I bought just for this kind of occasion...?!"

"Hold on, Ruri. You're jumping the gun a little."

"...! You're absolutely right. Thank you. I was so excited I got ahead of myself. The real ace in the hole isn't erotic lingerie, but neat white underwear."

"That isn't what I meant."

"You're always so cool and reserved, Hizumi. I'm so grateful, you know? You're always here for me, my good friend—"

"Could you put yourself in the shoes of this *good friend* for a minute?" Hizumi said in all seriousness, her expression sullen. "Why are you going on about underwear all of a sudden...? Why don't we start from the outside...? Hold on; is there really a chance he might *see* them...?"

"Well, you know... He's my brother... And it's not like he should have eyes for his own sister, but still..."

"H-how lewd..." Hizumi covered her mouth with her hands as her face turned bright red. She quickly shook her head as though to dispel unwanted thoughts. "How's this, Ruri? If this is what you want, I'll support you. But don't let yourself get carried away. You have to look after yourself, all right...?"

"Yep... Got it. I guess I'll go with gift catalogues with vouchers to give to the guests at our wedding instead of commemorative plates..."

"You're jumping the gun again!" Hizumi couldn't help but cry out loud.

That Saturday, at nine thirty in the morning—

"Here we go!"

Knight Ruri Fuyajoh, dressed in her finest clothes, set out from the Garden.

After completing all the formalities to leave the grounds, she passed through the main gate. Glancing over her shoulder, the huge school buildings and its various ancillary facilities that she had left behind just a moment earlier had been transformed now into a regular every-day school.

Of course, they hadn't really been transformed. Due to an illusion designed to conceal the Garden from *the outside*, they had simply been disguised as something else.

Returning her gaze to the road ahead, she let out a sigh to calm herself and started down the footpath.

Her destination was the plaza in front of the station, where she had agreed to meet Mushiki. From the Garden, it should take her around fifteen minutes to reach it. Their rendezvous was scheduled for ten o'clock, so she ought to have plenty of time to spare.

That said, she had to consciously slow her steps to keep from walking too fast. If she didn't, she would have ended up skipping along at a brisk pace.

Only that was understandable.

After all... Today she was going on a date with Mushiki.

"..."

She had to muster her iron will to suppress the bubbly feelings welling up inside her.

It wouldn't do to look too excited. If Mushiki saw her in such a state, he would end up taking advantage of her.

Exactly. That was that. This was this. While she might have accepted his invitation to go on a date, she was still committed to getting him kicked out of the Garden.

So she had to keep her cool today. No matter how much fun she was having, she couldn't let it show. She made sure to carve that thought into her mind.

However...

"..."

She walked for fifteen minutes with those thoughts jostling around in her head. Yet the second she spotted Mushiki at their arranged meeting place, she all but forgot her previous self-remonstrations as her heart skipped a beat.

No doubt having noticed her, Mushiki glanced her way. "Ruri!" he called out.

"…!"

She jumped in surprise but quickly feigned composure and adopted a moody pose.

"What's the matter now? You ought to be thanking me for even coming, no?"

Having heard that, Mushiki's eyes widened in surprise as he looked at her. "You're beautiful," he said. "You surprised me when I first saw you."

"…?!"

Ruri felt the blood rushing to her head, and she pulled away sharply at this unexpected compliment.

Not a second later, however, she slapped herself on the cheek to control her expression.

"R-Ruri?" Mushiki asked.

"Never mind. It was just a mosquito. Anyway, where are we going…?"

Before she could finish that question, she fell silent, blinking several times over.

There was another figure standing behind Mushiki—Saika's attendant, Kuroe Karasuma.

"Good morning," the plain-clothed Kuroe said with a short bow.

Ruri likewise bobbed her head in response. "Hmm? Ah, right. Hi."

Then, a few seconds later—

"Wait, whaaat?!" she screamed at the top of her lungs.

"Wh-what's wrong, Ruri?" Mushiki asked, pulling away at her sudden outcry.

"Isn't that *my* line?! What's Kuroe doing here?!"

"What…? Because we're going out together."

"Hah…?!" Ruri's eyes widened even more when she heard this.

"...What?" she began to mutter under her breath, her hands trembling. "What's the meaning of this...? *Together*...? A three-person date? Don't tell me he was into Kuroe, not me? Then why invite *me* here...? Is he just trying to flaunt some lovey-dovey relationship...?! No, no, no, you have to keep cool, Ruri Fuyajoh. A mage can't afford to lose her nerve... You've got to consider all the possibilities..."

She rested her hands on her forehead and fell to pondering with a serious look.

Mushiki couldn't make out what she was saying, but he understood at some vague level that she was taken aback by Kuroe's presence.

Although that didn't make any sense. Without Kuroe, today's investigation would have been impossible.

For a moment, he let his mind take him back to the conversation he'd had with Kuroe a few days earlier, just after the attack by the annihilation factors.

"There is a certain course of action only available to us now that we know the assailant is aware of Lady Saika's survival."

"A certain course of action...?"

"Yes. An investigation outside the walls of the Garden. Until now, we have remained within the Garden to try to keep Lady Saika's survival a secret from your assailant. However, if the truth has already been exposed, that strategy is rendered useless. So let's return to the site where she was attacked and examine any lingering traces of magical energy. Of course, we will need a knight to escort us..."

So when Mushiki had stumbled upon Ruri shortly after parting ways with Kuroe, he had asked her to join them. Kuroe had been unusually appreciative of his quick thinking.

Seeing Ruri's reaction now, Kuroe cupped her chin in her hand. "Hmm..." Then she slid across to Mushiki, leaning close to his ear. "You mentioned that you had convinced her to join us, but she doesn't seem entirely satisfied by this arrangement. In that case, there is nothing we can do about it. We shall have to set out alone, just the two of us."

"Huh?"

"What...?!"

Ruri's eyes snapped wide open at the sound of the word *alone*. "Wh-why would you say that?! I don't mind!"

"No, please, there's no need for you to go out of your way. I can escort my darling Mushiki—*ahem*—by myself."

"*Darling?!* Did you just call him your *darling?!*" Ruri cried in shock. After pulling at the roots of her hair, she leaped toward Mushiki and snatched him away. "All right, all right, got it! Argh, I don't get it! Let's just go already, all right?!" she said in a desperate tone.

Mushiki didn't exactly follow, but it looked like they were ready to go, so he breathed a sigh of relief. "Thank you. I was afraid you wouldn't want to join us," he said, flashing her a smile.

"Nggghhh!" Ruri let out a smothered cough.

"It looks like that worked," Kuroe said in a small voice as she watched from the sidelines.

"Kuroe... Why did you say that?" Mushiki asked in an equally low whisper.

"There seems to have been some misunderstanding," Kuroe explained. "She may have gone home if I didn't put on an act, so I decided to fan the flames a little."

"Ah, I see..."

"And also..."

"Yes?"

"Knight Fuyajoh's reaction *was* somewhat amusing."

"..."

Mushiki couldn't help but think *that* was the main reason behind her choice of words...but he tried to convince himself that he was just imagining things.

While the two of them were busy whispering back and forth, Ruri, it seemed, had managed to regain her composure and now turned her attention back to them.

"...So where are we going?" she asked. "To see a movie? The aquarium? Or maybe something adventurous, like an amusement park?"

"Huh?" Mushiki stared back at her blankly.

Ruri's lips twitched in disapproval. "Hah? So you invited me here with no plan at all? You really are hopeless, huh...?"

"N-no, I *do* have a plan. We're just not going anywhere like that today. We have somewhere more important to go."

"More important...?" Ruri muttered before suddenly choking up, her cheeks turning bright red, as though her thoughts had just led her to the wrong conclusion.

"I-it's a little too soon for *that*, no?! And Kuroe's here, too!"

"...? Yeah, we need her to join us for it."

"...! So you planned this from the beginning...? Er, you can't mean you want her to watch...?! Or that you want *me* to watch...?!" she exclaimed in confusion, breaking out in a sweat.

Mushiki tilted his head and reached out toward her. "What are you doing, Ruri? Let's go?"

"Huh? Ah, um, er..." With a hesitant nod, she took his hand in her own.

Her whole body was trembling all over.

At that moment, Mushiki realized something. She was trying to hold hands with him just like they used to as children.

"Ah, sorry. But you're a high schooler now."

"...! Wh-what does that matter?! If you want to hold hands, I'm not going to stop you!"

"No, I wasn't trying to—"

"Mushiki! I don't care! If you want to, I won't stop you!" Ruri shouted, emphasizing each and every word.

Mushiki could only watch on in bewilderment.

Kuroe, by his other side, acted natural, and as she took off at a walk, she said, "All right. Let's go."

"Ah, yeah."

"Wait for meee!" Ruri called after them as the two began to leave. "What...? Kuroe, what are you...?!"

"I've nothing more to say," Kuroe responded, her tone of voice as calm as could be.

"Ngh..." Ruri could only gnash her teeth in frustration. Even so, she seemed to quickly make up her mind, and as her face turned bright red, she grabbed Mushiki's right hand in her own. "L-let's go."

"Eh? Ah... Right."

So holding hands with Kuroe on his left and Ruri on his right, Mushiki began to make his way past the square in front of the station and down the main street.

Holding hands with not one but two girls was attracting considerable attention from passersby. Nonetheless, he was moved by the fact that he had finally managed to return to the outside world after what seemed like an eternity.

It had only been a few days, but it felt like forever since he had last laid eyes on the familiar scenery, the nostalgic cityscape. He found himself catching his breath as he looked up into the sky and savored the feeling of having returned home filling his lungs.

"...Ah," Ruri exclaimed after a few minutes, seemingly having spotted something.

At the end of her line of sight was a food truck that sold crepes.

"Well, if that's what you want, I suppose I'll share a crepe with you!" she declared.

"I didn't say anything... But do you want one?" Mushiki answered with a forced smile.

Ruri puffed out her cheeks. "Isn't it natural to stop for a bite to eat when you invite a girl out on a date?"

"...Huh? But you don't normally eat all that much when you're out on a survey, do you...?"

The two of them watched each other for a long moment, both similarly confused.

Well, Mushiki thought, if she wanted a snack that badly, he didn't have any good reason to refuse.

He glanced across at Kuroe, as though asking permission. Having understood his unvoiced question, she nodded, her gaze fixed on the ground ahead of her.

"All right. We're here, so we might as well get something."

"Really?!"

Ruri's face lit up at once—before quickly turning grim again as she let out a huff. "W-well... We might as well, no? I mean, you're going to be leaving the Garden soon anyway, so let's treat it as a farewell gift. A last supper of sorts."

Mushiki felt strangely on edge. "Where did that come from...? Anyway, what flavors do you two want?"

"...Strawberries and cream."

"I'll have banana and chocolate."

Ruri and Kuroe said simultaneously as they both looked over the menu.

"Hmm. I guess I'll go with strawberries and cream, too," Mushiki said after giving it a little thought.

"...!" Ruri struck a victorious pose at this decision before peering at Kuroe with a look of triumph. "I knew it! Even if we haven't seen each other in years, we're still brother and sister, right? Maybe we have similar tastes? I'm sure we've got so much in common."

"..." Kuroe said nothing in response, her face expressionless... But for some reason, she looked slightly annoyed.

"Er, um... Right, I'm ordering, then."

After paying at the counter and receiving the crepes, the three of them sat at a nearby bench. Ruri on the right, Kuroe on the left, and Mushiki sandwiched in between.

"Well, let's dig in..."

He took a bite of his crepe, the spongy wrap filled with strawberries and whipped cream. The blend of rich sweetness and refreshing tartness created a perfect harmony in his mouth.

"Hmm... It's been a while since I last had a crepe. It tastes pretty good, huh?" he said.

"Yep." Ruri nodded. "And it's even more delicious eating it here with my brother!"

"Huh?"

"I said you should give up on becoming a mage and drop out of the Garden."

"What? That wasn't what I heard, though?"

Mushiki was visibly confused—but at that moment, Kuroe, chewing on a bite of her banana-and-chocolate crepe, glanced his way. "Hmm.

I wonder what that one tastes like. Do you want to swap for a minute, Mushiki?"

"Ah, okay. Here you go." He held out his crepe, letting her take a bite.

Then Kuroe, likewise, offered him a taste of her own.

"Wh-whaaaaaat?!" Ruri screamed like a character in some horror comic.

"Whoa. You surprised me there. What's wrong, Ruri?"

"That's *my* line! How can you be doing that like it's so natural?! I mean, it's...it's basically...you know?!" she exclaimed, pointing back and forth between Mushiki and Kuroe.

"Ah," Mushiki let out after a long moment, his eyes widening in realization. "Now that you mention it..."

"Hmm. But there's no point making a fuss over a little indirect kiss after all we've done together," Kuroe said matter-of-factly.

"All we've done together?! All we've done together?!" Ruri gasped, her eyes swirling dangerously.

"Why worry about a light drizzle after you've just gone for a swim in the lake?" Kuroe asked her.

"Can you stop with the suggestive metaphors?!" Ruri screamed. "Nggghhh..." She groaned in frustration before holding out her own crepe. "Here, Mushiki! Take a bite of mine!"

"Huh...? But they're the same flavor."

"What...?!" Ruri let out a silent gasp. "Y-you planned this, Kuroe...!"

"What a rude accusation," Kuroe said with an unreadable glower.

Ruri, however, paid her no more attention, stuffing what remained of her crepe into her mouth and running back to the van to buy a fresh one.

Then, after taking a bite of her second one, she held it out to Mushiki. "It's tropical mango! You can't complain about this one, can you...?!"

"Um, I guess not..."

Feeling like he had little choice in the matter, Mushiki took a small bite of the new crepe.

"...Hee-hee-hee." Ruri chuckled as she, too, took another mouthful.

"..."

Mushiki did worry that she was eating a little too much...but the innocent smile she flashed him brought back fond memories.

◇

After spending a good three hours walking a route that should have taken no more than thirty minutes without distractions, Mushiki and the others finally arrived at the park next to their destination.

Apart from some time spent window-shopping and taking some photo stickers at the game arcade, the trip had been largely uneventful.

The three of them sat side by side on a park bench sipping at some iced tea they had bought from a vending machine.

"...Kuroe. I was walking down an alley near here when I wound up in some strange world," Mushiki whispered softly in her ear so Ruri wouldn't overhear them.

Giving him a small nod of understanding, Kuroe quickly rose to her feet. "Ruri, I need to find a restroom. I'll be back in a minute."

"Ah, okay. We'll wait here, then."

"Very well," Kuroe said before glancing toward Mushiki.

Sensing her intentions, Mushiki decided to follow her lead. "Ah, I'll go, too," he said, rising from the bench.

"Huh? You too? Have you had too much tea? Are you feeling all right? Are you giving up on becoming a mage?" Ruri asked inquisitively.

Her obsession with him leaving the Garden had practically become a fixed tagline at the end of her sentences.

Mushiki let out a forced chuckle as he waved his hands, before taking off in the direction of the public restrooms with Kuroe by his side—and then ducking quietly into the shadows.

Then, a little quicker on their feet, the two of them headed toward their real destination.

"Is it really safe to leave Ruri like this?" Mushiki asked.

"It *is* a risk, but we can't afford to let her see the scene of the crime, so it can't be helped. Let's wrap this up quickly so we can go back," Kuroe answered.

Mushiki nodded as they made their way down the street.

It wasn't long before the familiar alleyway opened up before him.

"It was around here, I believe?" Kuroe came to a stop, glancing around.

Mushiki's eyes opened wide in surprise. "How did you know?"

"Just a hunch," Kuroe answered as if it was a matter of course.

The alleyway was situated roughly halfway between his old school and his home and was most certainly the same area he had entered before getting lost in that urban labyrinth. It was a bit of a distance from the downtown area, so there weren't any pedestrians around, only the sound of the wind rustling through the nearby trees.

At first glance, it looked like an ordinary alley... But maybe Kuroe had another way of scanning it that remained as of yet unknown to him.

"..."

Kuroe glanced carefully around, then slowly fell to her knees and let her fingertips graze softly against the asphalt.

"We will need to examine the area in detail. Mushiki, give me a hand."

"Right. What do you want me to do?"

No sooner did he finish speaking than Kuroe stood up, her pace brisk as she pushed him against a nearby wall.

"Um, Kuroe...? Are you...?"

"Precisely. Once you've changed into Lady Saika's form, disperse the magical energy around you. With that catalyst, you can check for any remaining traces that were left behind on the same wavelength. That should help us to zero in on any traces of the fourth substantiation used at the time."

"But there must have been all kinds of comings and goings here since then... Besides, Ruri is waiting for us, and once I transform, it isn't exactly easy to change back."

"Don't worry about that. You're remarkably simple to deal with."

"How rude."

"No more grumbling, please. Open your mouth. I'll turn you into a girl."

"That could be easily misconstrued—*ngh*..."

Before he could finish his sentence, Kuroe pulled him down by the collar and initiated a forceful kiss.

All at once, a warmth took hold of his body, his skin radiating a faint glow... And with that, he became Saika. The clothes he was wearing, being woven from spirit thread, likewise adjusted to a women's fit.

"The Witch of Resplendent Color, Saika Kuozaki, will descend upon the world tonight," Mushiki said.

"...What kind of embarrassing quip is that?" Kuroe asked.

"I—I just thought it would be cool to have a catchphrase or something."

"There's no need... Now, let's get started. Stand in the middle of the road here."

"Right. Um... How do I disperse the magical energy, though?"

"As I've told you before, you have yet to bring your powers under control, Mushiki, and are constantly releasing small amounts of magical energy. It will be enough for you just to stand right there as you are. Just try not to do anything unnecessary. We wouldn't want a repeat of what happened in the classroom the other day."

"Hmm," he murmured as he approached the designated spot, adopting a fancy model-like pose.

"Standing normally will be fine," Kuroe said flatly.

"Huh? But—"

"Normal will be fine."

Mushiki's shoulders slumped in disappointment. *He* had thought it would look cool.

"In that case, let's begin." Kuroe raised a hand in front of her, took a deep breath, and then chanted, "First Substantiation: Eye of Inquiry."

With that, a crest spread around her neck like a collar, her eyes flashing with an inner light.

"...! Kuroe! Is that...?"

"A magical technique to analyze the composition and structure of targeted objects. I am, after all, a mage of the Garden."

As she spoke, her dimly glowing eyes took in the area around her.

"Tra-la-la-la, tra-la-la-la... ♪"

Sitting on the park bench, Ruri was humming a happy tune to herself as she shook her bottle of cold tea.

There was nothing unexpected about that. After all, she was out on a date with Mushiki.

How many years had it been since she had last gone exploring with him? This must have been their first time since she was in elementary school.

It wasn't like they were doing anything important today—just walking around town, stopping to get something to eat, and doing a little shopping. However, the mere addition of a little spice to her life—Mushiki—had been enough to make everything refreshingly, irresistibly fun. In fact, she had been looking forward to this so much that she had barely been able to get any sleep the past few days since receiving his invitation.

"...Hmm, no, wait. Calm down, calm down...," she muttered under her breath as she shook her head.

Yes, it was certainly true that she was having a good time on her date with Mushiki. Still, that didn't mean she could permit him to remain at the Garden. If she let it show just how happy she was, he might not take her objections seriously.

She clapped her cheeks in self-remonstration, then glanced back to the clock in the middle of the park.

"Huh? They're taking their time...," she muttered.

It would be a violation of basic etiquette to go snooping on them while they were both using the restroom, and normally, she would hardly worry about anything like this.

However, the fact that the two of them had both decided to go at the exact same time *did* have her a little on edge.

"...Th-they couldn't..."

At that moment, an unpleasant vision took hold of her brain.

She envisioned that Mushiki and Kuroe had both made their way toward the public restroom, but when the two of them were out of her sight, Kuroe licked her lips and looked at Mushiki with lewd smile.

"I'll be back in a minute, Kuroe."

"Oh-ho-ho... Whatever are you talking about, Mushiki? We've finally got some time alone, just the two of us."

"Huh?! Wh-what are you doing, Kuroe?! Ruri's just around the corner...!"

"Don't worry. I can't stand it, watching the two of you being lovey-dovey all day. Come here. I'll teach you what real pleasure feels like."

"Wha—?! Help, Ruri! Heeelp! Ruriii!"

"Damn you, Kuroe! Get your hands off my brother...!"

Ruri's eyes widened as she crushed the plastic bottle in her hand and took off with explosive force.

"..."

Roughly three minutes after deploying her first substantiation, Kuroe squinted and lowered her hands.

In perfect sync, the crest that had appeared around her neck like-wise dissipated.

"Did you find anything, Kuroe?" Mushiki asked.

"...Yes. I detected Lady Saika's residual magical energy. It seems this is definitely where the incident took place. Fourth substantiation techniques are used to create their own miniature planes of existence, but they always have a starting point here in the real world." Despite that response, her tone and expression were stiff. "However, I can't detect any other traces of magical energy. Of course, I can sense weak amounts of mana, ubiquitous throughout the world, but nothing to suggest that a fourth substantiation was deployed..."

"Does that mean the perpetrator covered his tracks...? Or that they didn't use a fourth substantiation in the first place...?" Mushiki asked.

Kuroe stroked her chin before responding. "The former, if I had to guess... It's hard to imagine the latter situation, given the circumstances. However, it's equally hard to imagine using enough power to trigger a fourth substantiation and then erasing all trace of that... And there is something else here that is bothering me."

"What's that?"

"Lady Saika's residual magical energy is unusually dense. I can only assume that she was in the midst of deploying her own fourth substantiation."

"...Hold on; are you saying she was trying to use it against her attacker? And that whoever it was then got her and erased all evidence of the fact?"

"That wouldn't be possible," Kuroe said brusquely with a shake of her head. "If she *had* deployed her fourth substantiation, there is no way she could have lost."

"...Right."

He thought back to his duel with Anviet, then to what had happened during the attack by the annihilation factors, and broke out in a sweat.

"But in that case...what on earth happened?"

"...That is indeed the question. There is one possibility—"

But at that moment—

"Mushikiii! Kuroeee!"

Behind them, from the direction of the park, came a deafening cry followed by the sound of thunderous footsteps.

"Is that...Ruri?"

"...! Madam Witch?!"

By the time Mushiki turned around, Ruri was already running toward him. No doubt startled to see him—or rather, Saika—she slammed on the brakes and came to a quick stop. There were faint skid marks behind her, and smoke was rising from her feet.

"It's an honor to bump into you in a place like this! What are you doing out and about today, Madam Witch?!" she said with a bow.

Mushiki did his best to give her a vague smile. "A-ah. I decided to go out for a walk for a change. What brings you here, Ruri?"

Only then did Ruri let out a labored breath as though suddenly remembering something. "Right...! Madam Witch, have you seen my brother and Kuroe around here? I mean... Ah, you probably don't know him... Er, he's a boy, and Kuroe looks like she'll take advantage of him! And something about that just triggers my maternal instincts! I have to find them!"

"Huh? Oh... Um...?"

It sounded like she had come looking for the two of them. Wondering how best to answer, Mushiki looked to Kuroe—only to find she had disappeared.

Looking carefully, he spotted her lurking behind a fence some distance away. She must have hidden herself the second she had sensed Ruri approaching.

This called for an immediate decision. There was no denying that things would have been even more complicated if Kuroe, who was supposed to have gone to the bathroom, had instead been standing beside him.

"..." Kuroe attempted a silent gesture his way. Mushiki could only interpret it as the words *Brush her off.*

"Ah, Kuroe? I saw her a moment ago. Um...yes, I think she said something about finding a convenience store because the restroom in the park was so crowded...?"

"...! R-really?!" Ruri exhaled loudly in relief. "So I *was* overthinking it... I was so sure of it..."

"So sure of what?"

"Ah! N-nothing!" Ruri shook her head, her cheeks bright red.

Mushiki glanced over at Kuroe once more. This time, her hands seemed to be saying *I'll join you later, so buy us some time.* Apparently, she had something else she wanted to look into.

"Um... Ruri. If you don't mind, how about you join me for a short while?"

"Huh?! A-are you sure?!"

"Yes. I'm a little tired after all that walking. I was just about to take a break. But I don't want to interrupt you if you're busy."

"It's no interruption! P-please come this way!" Ruri seemed fearful but thankful at the same time as she motioned toward the park.

With that, Mushiki followed beside her as they made their way there at a slow pace.

"Could you wait here a moment, please...?" Ruri said once they arrived...before spreading a handkerchief on a bench in the shade of a tree.

"Please, after you," she said, gesturing.

"A-ah. Thank you."

It was a bit too much, but he felt guilty disrespecting the hospitality she was extending to him, so he availed himself of her kindness.

Nonetheless, even after he took the seat on the bench, Ruri continued to stand directly in front of him.

Sensing her intention to wait on him, Mushiki showed her a gentle smile. "Oh-ho, do sit down, Ruri. You'll make me feel uncomfortable doing that."

"...! M-my apologies..." With a look of utmost embarrassment, she sat beside him, her back straight.

The depths of her respect for Saika must have been considerable, Mushiki mused. He couldn't help but break into a smile as he watched her.

"Madam Witch...?"

"Oh. No, it's nothing... How have you been today? It's unusual for you to go out and about with Kuroe, no?"

Needless to say, Mushiki was fully aware of the situation. However, he would have to make sure that Ruri relayed it all to Saika for the conversation to proceed smoothly, so he made a point of asking her about her day.

Ruri blushed, scratching nervously at her cheek. "Ah... Well, to tell you the truth... Hee-hee-hee... I'm on a date with my brother...," she said shyly.

"Huh?" He stared back wide-eyed.

"Is something the matter?" Ruri tilted her head.

"Ah, no. Not at all." Mushiki shook his head in an attempt to brush his question aside.

The two of them had seemed to be talking at cross-purposes since morning, but to think things had gotten so misconstrued...

"Ah... So that's why you looked to be having so much fun, Ruri."

"Huh? Is it that obvious?! Uh-oh, this isn't good..." With that, Ruri began to rub her cheeks with her hands, as though hoping to change her facial expression.

"...? *What* isn't good? If you're enjoying yourself, you ought to let it show, no?"

"No, I can't. I *am* enjoying myself... But I can't let my brother know that."

"...? Why not?" Mushiki asked.

Ruri wore a troubled expression. "Well... While you were absent from class, we had two new transfer students join us... The first was Kuroe, and the second was Mushiki Kuga—my brother from the *outside*. I don't know how on earth he found out about the Garden..."

"Ah... Is that so?" he answered vaguely.

After all, it would be unusual for the headmistress not to know about any new transfer students, and Kuroe was, after all, Saika's own attendant. It would be best not to pretend that this was entirely new information.

"So I... It's hard for me to ask this of the head of the Garden... But I really don't want my brother to be a mage..."

"...Hmm," Mushiki hummed, crossing his arms. He already knew that. "Do you...dislike your brother, Ruri?"

"Not at all!" she cried back.

She immediately adopted a frightened look and shrugged. "S-sorry..."

"No, it's fine. But can you tell me why?" Mushiki asked.

Ruri looked conflicted but, making up her mind, began to speak: "It's a simple reason. Annihilation factors are capable of destroying the whole world, and the damage they cause is enormous. It isn't unusual for even relatively small annihilation factors to cause deaths numbering in the thousands in the blink of an eye. If they can be defeated within the window for reversible annihilation, that damage can be made like it never happened... But any mage who sees it for themselves will still be injured. And there's no way to undo death then... I can't lie to you, Madam Witch. As shameful as it is, that's the honest truth. I don't want my brother to get hurt. I don't want to lose him. I mean—I became a mage to protect him."

"..." Mushiki was at a loss for words at this confession.

"I know that once you've entered the Garden, you'll see an annihilation factor," Ruri continued, her gaze burning with determination. "But it can't be too late. There *has* to be a way. If we can block his access to magic and erase his memories, he should still be able to go back to the outside world. I'm glad he followed me all the way to the Garden, but I can't... I can't..." She fell silent, clenching her fists tightly.

She seemed to stumble over her words toward the end there... But maybe that was just his imagination.

"I know you can't just ignore his wishes. But I'll make sure he accepts it. When he does, I'll do anything for your help." With that, she looked straight into his eyes.

"..."

Mushiki stifled his urge to speak. He felt like he was being compelled to action by Ruri's sheer strength of will.

His words right now wouldn't be those of the real Saika. He couldn't speak for her on a matter of such importance.

After giving it some thought, he let out a deep sigh. "That must have been a slip of the tongue just now. Ruri...I can see you really do love your brother."

"Yes! I do!" she replied with a brilliant smile, completely at odds with her prior demeanor.

"Ruri."

"Yes! What is it?"

"Can I hug you? Just a little?"

"Of course— Huh?!" Her face turned bright red as she flew into a panic.

Mushiki had spoken too quickly out of love, but he was, after all, presently inhabiting Saika's body. Ruri's confession just now must have hit him too strongly. With a wave of his hand, he said, "I'm sorry. Don't worry about it. I suppose I just got a little emotional."

"N-not at all..." Ruri looked relieved, but at the same time, somehow disappointed.

Then she suddenly jolted upright, glancing around quickly.

"Ruri? What's wrong?"

"Ah... I just thought it's about time those two came back... Madam Witch, please don't tell Mushiki what I said. If he knew, I'm sure he would absolutely refuse to leave the Garden."

"...Ah. I won't say anything... Not a word."

"Please. Ah, and the same for Kuroe. Those two seem to be really close for some reason..." She stopped there, looking like she had suddenly remembered something. "Oh, and about Kuroe, Madam Witch... There's something I've been wondering for a while now..."

"Hmm? What would that be?"

"When exactly did you hire her?"

"...Huh?"

Mushiki's throat constricted in alarm at that question.

"What do you mean? *When did I hire her...?*"

"Yes. I mean, you've never had an attendant before, right?"

"...?! What...?!"

He realized at once it was a very un-Saika-like reaction, but for a few brief seconds, he was unable to compose himself. Fully aware that his last question made absolutely no sense spoken from Saika's lips, he hastened to add: "Hold on a minute. Kuroe has been serving in the mansion, right?"

"...? Was that it? I'm sorry, Madam Witch. I've visited countless times, but I never saw her before."

"..." As he listened to her go on, Mushiki's heart began to race.

He was well aware of Ruri's earnest and persistent personality and had come to appreciate over the past few days how painfully devoted she was to Saika.

Which was why he couldn't stop a certain thought from coming to mind.

Was it really possible that Ruri was completely unaware of Saika's attendant, who assisted her in every aspect of life?

Was this simply an oversight on her part?

Had Saika gone to lengths to conceal Kuroe's existence?

Or else...

Several possibilities swirled through his head. With a trembling voice, he asked, "Ruri, when *did* you first learn about Kuroe?"

She placed her finger against her cheek as though probing her memories. "Well, the first time I saw her...was at the last regular meeting. You brought her with you to the conference room, then, right?"

"..." Once more, Mushiki was left speechless.

The day of the regular meeting. He remembered it well.

After all, it was the very same day when he had merged with Saika and woken up in the Garden.

...And before that day, Ruri hadn't so much as laid eyes on Kuroe.

Was that to say that Kuroe had only come to the mansion *after* he and Saika were attacked...?

If that was true...

How had she established herself in Saika's mansion?

How had she seemed to know everything about his situation?

How was she guiding his every action?

Who on earth was she?

"It can't be..." Mushiki moaned as a cold premonition took root in his stomach.

If he said any more, there would be no going back. He understood that perfectly, but he had to ask. Already, his mouth was putting into words the worst possible scenario.

"Kuroe, are you—?"

At that moment, as though to cut him off midspeech, the scenery around them *changed*.

"What...?!"

"...!"

It was a strange feeling, as though darkness was flooding the beautiful afternoon park.

That darkness enveloped the area instantly, and several huge structures suddenly emerged from the ground.

An urban labyrinth with no end in sight. A gray world comprised of iron and stone.

Yes, there could be no mistaking it—this was the eerie space into which Mushiki had wandered that day.

"...! A fourth substantiation...?! But who could be—?!" Ruri choked on her words for a moment—but her expression quickly took on that of a warrior.

No doubt she had realized what this was. They had already brought it up at the general meeting a few days earlier. This was the mysterious mage who had attacked Saika.

"Luminous Blade!" she chanted, two lapis lazuli–colored crests glowing atop her head as a *naginata* comprised entirely of light materialized in her hand. Her second substantiation, with the rank of *matter*.

Ruri braced herself with her sword—and as if in response to her defensive posture, several human-shaped shadows crawled out from amid the towering structures that had appeared around them.

When she saw this, she glowered. "Annihilation Factor No. 414: Wraith. Still, how can there be annihilation factors within a fourth substantiation...?"

The shadows offered no answer. They turned their unreadable countenances toward Ruri and Mushiki, then threw themselves forward in one lunge.

"Hah!" With a frenzied cry, Ruri lashed out with her blade of light.

As she moved, that weapon stretched long and thin like a thread of string.

Then, as if imbued with a will of its own, it fanned out in all directions, effortlessly slicing through the amassing shadows that continued to surround them.

Defeated, those figures faded into thin air without even having time to let out a final gasp.

But even after overcoming those creatures, Ruri and Mushiki were still trapped in the gray labyrinth.

"Tch... Just because we stepped foot outside the Garden, *someone* thinks they can mess around with us," Ruri said with a click of her tongue before raising her voice as though calling to someone atop the towering edifices nearby. "Whoever you are in charge of this plane, come out! A mage who's reached their fourth substantiation ought to be capable of more than just that last stingy assault! What are you trying to achieve? Do you even know who you just attacked?"

Her call echoed across the walls of the myriad buildings, like the rumbling voice of a mountain deity.

Then, as if in response, a soft pitter-patter of footsteps began to sound from deep within the darkness.

"...! Ruri!" Mushiki called out in warning.

"I know," she said with a small nod, holding her *naginata* at the ready.

Finally, a lone figure stepped out from the gap between two tangled buildings.

They were covered from head to toe in a dark robe, their face concealed by a hood that obscured their appearance and age—even whether they were a man or a woman.

Nonetheless, the four-layered crest floating above their head in a sharp, piercing design akin to a wide-brimmed hat clearly indicated that they were the master of this plane.

"You've finally decided to show yourself. In the name of the Knights of the Garden, you're under—"

Ruri, still holding her *naginata* at the approaching figure, choked on her words.

"Ruri?" Mushiki asked, looking at her in concern.

That was only natural. After all, though she had until that moment been staring calmly toward their enemy, Ruri's face was now tinged with indescribable dismay and consternation.

Sweat dripped down her face, her lips quivering silently. Her eyes had opened wider than he had ever seen before, her gaze wavering—and, it seemed, slightly out of focus.

"You...," emerged a gravelly sound from deep in her throat.

Those words. Her voice.

She must have realized just who their opponent truly was.

"...Ruri!" Mushiki called out.

"..."

The approaching mage lifted an arm into the air—a slender, beautiful hand poking out from their sleeve.

Then the figure snapped their fingers.

"...?!"

All of a sudden, the glowing blade in Ruri's hands swelled in size, a thousand needles erupting from it to pierce her hands, her legs, her chest.

"Ugh..."

Unable to even process what had just happened, she choked on her words as she sank to the ground, an ocean of blood spewing from her body.

It had all happened in the blink of an eye.

"Ruriii!" Mushiki screamed, running to her side as she collapsed in a pool of blood.

A second later, the crest above her head faded away, and the *naginata* in her hands vanished in a flash of light.

She was barely breathing, and it was clear that she was in critical condition. Blood continued to pour from the countless wounds that covered her body. Among them, one of those light-based needles that had pierced her chest seemed to have hit a vital organ. She needed immediate treatment, lest her injuries prove fatal. But even then, it might not be enough...

"...Ugh..."

The tragic sight of his sister bleeding out tore at Mushiki's heart.

Searing rage and enmity building up inside him, he glared across at the mage standing before them.

"You...!"

The unforgivable enemy who had attacked Saika, mortally wounded him, and now dealt a fatal injury to his precious sister.

...He had to defeat this foe. Here and now.

If he didn't, Ruri would die. Saika would die. *He* would die.

He understood how impossible this task seemed. Even so, having made up his mind, he rose to his feet and lifted his hands toward the mage.

"...Heh."

Having seen his state, and after one exhalation of breath, the mage turned on their heel.

As if to say they had accomplished their goal for the day.

Or perhaps even that Mushiki wasn't worth their time.

"Wait—," Mushiki began before swallowing his words.

No, he couldn't let this enemy get away with everything that they had done. But what would happen to Ruri if their foe turned back around?

He couldn't risk Ruri's life in a moment of recklessness when he didn't have the faintest hope of emerging victorious. Digging his fingernails into his palms and biting his lip in frustration, he stared at the mage's back as the figure walked away, vanishing into the darkness.

A moment later, the labyrinthine landscape that had enveloped them all crumbled away, and the peaceful, late-afternoon park returned to take its place.

One thing, however, had most certainly changed.

"...Arrrggghhh..."

Unable to contain his rage, clenching his fists smeared with his sister's blood, he cried out into the heavens.

Chapter 5
⇥ Witch ⇤

That evening, in the headmistress's office on the top floor of the central school building, Mushiki received a report from Erulka on Ruri's condition.

"...That's the situation. She lost a lot of blood, but fortunately, it isn't life-threatening. Of course, there's no telling what might have happened if you had brought her to us any later," she concluded, tapping the clipboard in her free hand.

Mushiki, listening from the table at the far end of the office, let out a sigh of relief.

After the attack, he had immediately reached out to the Garden to have Ruri transported to the medical building for emergency care. To be perfectly honest, he had been unable to relax all day until hearing this report.

Nonetheless, his situation was such that he couldn't rest easy for long. He clenched his jaw, his expression grim.

Erulka must have sensed his unease, as she folded her arms in front of her and said, "What the hell happened, Saika? It's unthinkable that Ruri could end up so badly injured."

"..." Mushiki, however, had no answer to offer.

He *couldn't* answer her.

At long last, Erulka let out a resigned sigh. "So you won't tell me...? Very well. I know you. You wouldn't keep your mouth shut without good reason."

"...Sorry."

"I said it's fine. Fill me in when you're ready." With that, she turned to leave the room.

"Erulka," Mushiki called out after her.

"Hmm?"

"My attendant...Kuroe. Did you know about her?" he asked.

Erulka tilted her head in suspicion. "Attendant... That girl in black? The first time I saw her was during the last general meeting. Is that what you mean?"

"...I see." Mushiki fell silent for a few seconds, then shook his head slightly. "Look after Ruri for me, Erulka," he said in a soft voice.

"Hmm. Leave her in my care," she said with a nod before leaving the office.

As the door closed behind her, the room was doused in cold silence.

"..."

Mushiki rose slowly to his feet and approached the mirror at the back of the chamber, staring at the figure reflected before him.

There, illuminated by the moonlight streaming in through the window, stood a young woman of immeasurable beauty.

Saika Kuozaki. The most powerful mage in the world and the head of the Garden. Mushiki's first great love.

And now—Mushiki himself.

She had met him, entrusted him with her body and strength, and given him this surreal double life.

All to defeat the mysterious figure who had attacked her.

To find a way to restore Saika's own mind and will.

Not once had he forgotten his purpose, nor neglected it. He had done everything within his power.

Yet this had been the result.

He had known from the beginning how reckless this was, had understood right from the get-go how unreasonable.

Perhaps he had let a little blind optimism take root in the corner of his mind. It would have been a lie to say he felt no surge of elation at the realization that he now possessed a previously unknown power of magic that continued to grow in potency by the day. There had been an unfounded confidence deep inside him that the body of his beloved Saika, with all its strength and ability, would be able to find a way to break through this predicament.

Now, however, he found himself overcome by an impossible sense of helplessness and self-loathing.

There was nothing he could do about it. He was clearly, conclusively, lacking.

He was possessed by a delusional compulsion to avenge Saika's death.

"...Ah..."

But not right now.

For the first time, he had faced his enemy directly, only for Ruri to get hurt. A flame of determination and resolve had been lit in his heart.

How dare she harm Ruri, his sweet little sister.

How dare she hurt Saika, the target of his affections.

"I'll never forgive you," he murmured softly, forcefully.

He then stepped forward and placed his hands on the mirror.

"Saika, I'm sorry about this. I'm about to do something reckless again," he said, his voice ringing with resolve. "Please lend me your strength."

With that, he gently placed his lips against it.

Outside the door at the back of the headmistress's room was an expansive garden.

Paved paths ran the length and breadth of the space, filled with well-maintained flower beds and copses of trees. It was late, with most of the illumination coming from the lampposts spread at even intervals.

Mushiki was on the top floor of the central school building. There was no way this scene could be literally beyond his door. Yet through magic, various doors in the Garden were mysteriously interconnected.

He hadn't known how to use the door at first and had ended up barging into several unintended destinations. Now, however, he was gradually getting used to it. Having confirmed that the passage did indeed lead where he wanted to go, he stepped inside and closed the door behind him.

It was the front yard outside Saika's mansion, in the northern precinct of the Garden. With that grand structure looming in the background, he slowly made his way forward.

"..."

As he reached the center of the grounds, the girl standing there waiting for him turned toward him.

"Mushiki, how is Knight Ruri's condition?" asked the girl—Kuroe Karasuma—with her usual expressionless countenance.

It should have been strange to find her standing by herself in a place like this, but Mushiki wasn't the least surprised.

After all, it was none other than he himself who had summoned her here.

Yes, he had something he had to make sure of, something to confirm.

"...Yes. It sounds like she'll make it," Mushiki answered, a slight numbness building in the pit of his stomach.

"I see. I'm glad to hear that... I was surprised to see them attack so boldly and in such numbers. There's no time to spare. We'll have to confront them directly. Please ready yourself, Mushiki," Kuroe said in a matter-of-fact tone.

Mushiki fixed her with a long stare before letting out a thin breath. "I...," he began.

"Yes?" Kuroe tilted her head quizzically.

"I'm grateful to you, Kuroe...," he continued, without averting his gaze. "After I was attacked by this *enemy* and merged with Saika, I didn't know up from down, but you were always there to give me a helping hand. If not for you, I'm sure I would have encountered a lot more problems than I did."

"There's no need to let that trouble you. I'm Lady Saika's attendant, after all," Kuroe said, standing up straight.

Even now, she was still playing her role to perfection.

Mushiki caught his breath. "So I want you to answer me honestly. Please."

"...? What are you talking—?"

"Kuroe. Who are you *really*?"

The moment those words left his lips, Kuroe snapped silent.

With that unreadable expression, she peered deep into Mushiki's face.

"...Saika never had an attendant," he continued slowly. He could feel his heart beating faster, but he fought to keep his panic under wraps. "Kuroe. You appeared here in the Garden at the same time I did... So I'll ask you again. Who are you? What were you trying to accomplish, taking on the name of Saika's attendant and deceiving me?"

Given the information he currently possessed, he had no intention of directly accusing her of being the assailant. A part of him still hoped she wasn't.

However, it was clear she was hiding *something* from him. That much was certain.

He needed answers.

"..." Kuroe remained silent for a long moment after this declaration.

Finally, a faint exhale seemed to rasp from her throat—

"Huh. So you figured it out?"

Her lips twisted into a ferocious grin.

"...!"

Her expression and tone were unrecognizable, causing every hair on Mushiki's body to stand on end.

She hadn't *changed*, exactly. There was no monster that had emerged from her back. It was just that her voice and mannerisms were vaguely off.

Yet he couldn't help but feel that the girl standing before him was now a completely different person.

"Who...who *are* you...?!" Mushiki tensed, bracing himself as he adopted a fighting posture.

Kuroe, watching, let out an amused laugh. "Yep, not a bad reaction there. Well, it's far from perfect, but still..."

At that moment, her figure seemed to blur, a different form appearing before him.

"Wha—?"

She practically teleported his way—no, she must have simply dashed toward him faster than the eye could see. There was no way he could match her speed and movements.

He hurried to activate his magical abilities, but he was too slow. She had already appeared closer even than his outstretched hands.

With that same momentum, she slammed her body into him, throwing him backward.

"Gah...!"

He was knocked flat onto his back on the hard pavement. Flustered, he glanced back up—only for a new question to spark inside his mind.

He might have been caught off guard, but he seemed to have sustained surprisingly little damage.

Yes, he had received a hard blow, and his back hurt where he had hit the ground, but that was about it. If Kuroe had been meaning to truly harm him, then this wouldn't be nearly enough.

At that moment—

"...?!"

His thoughts were interrupted.

Because behind Kuroe, right where he had been standing a moment ago, a huge upside-down spire now stretched out from high up in the sky.

"Huh...? What...?!"

The spire pierced the ground, scattering chunks of earth and sending shock waves coursing through the surrounding area. Mushiki looked over Kuroe's shoulder with a sense of surreality at the scene unfolding before him.

"...Good grief... Always with the flashy theatrics..." She let out a deep breath as she looked over her shoulder and took in the towering edifice.

Then, as though having been waiting for that very moment, the upside-down spire piercing the center of the courtyard flashed with light, a dazzling burst of brilliance flooding Mushiki's vision.

By the time it subsided, the landscape around him, the world in which he and Kuroe now found themselves, had become unrecognizable.

"No..."

Once more, he found himself in an inorganic urban labyrinth comprised of innumerable towering structures.

As he took in the eerie view for the third time, his breath caught in his throat.

"What's the meaning of this? Aren't *you* the enemy, Kuroe...?"

"...Hah? Well... I thought a little surprise might prove interesting...," she said with a thin smile. Her expression, however, remained deathly pale.

Only then did Mushiki notice it. Her back was wet with blood.

She had done more than just push him to safety. She had sensed an oncoming projectile falling from the sky and had thrown herself before him to act as a human shield.

"...! Kuroe! You're bleeding!"

"...A poor shot, huh...? But you had better focus on keeping your eyes sharp. She's here... The worst reaper of them all..." With those words, Kuroe lost all strength.

She fainted and was still breathing, but she was losing a lot of blood. She needed medical treatment immediately.

Mushiki soon realized just how impossible that would prove to be.

Seemingly in response to her final words, a figure appeared, slowly seeping out from the darkness.

A robe shrouded their entire body, the hood allowing a glimpse of only the figure's mouth.

Whoever they were, the figure was clearly reluctant to reveal their identity, with only four brilliant crests shining radiantly above their head.

"..."

There could be no doubt about it. This was the same detestable mage who had mortally wounded Saika, pierced Mushiki's chest, and attacked Ruri earlier today.

"A-ahhhhhhhhh!"

No sooner did he recognize the figure than Mushiki clenched his right hand high up in front of him.

Above his head, his own crest expanded, an angelic halo in the shape of a witch's hat.

His first substantiation. A technique designed to extract and express only phenomena from his present waking world.

He had been unable to properly control it in class a few days ago, but he had activated it now with ease.

Around him, several spheres of light came into being.

With a sweeping motion, he sent those orbs careering toward the mage at tremendous speed.

"..."

Just before he could land the hit, they veered sharply away, changing trajectory as if repulsed, before exploding behind the mage with a rain of fireworks.

"How...?"

Mushiki stared wide-eyed as he took in the absurd scene.

That was only natural. The mage had neither blocked the attack nor deflected it. Rather, his projectiles seemed to change course entirely on their own, as though refusing to inflict harm on their target.

Mushiki was left stunned by this inexplicable phenomenon.

"It's useless," the mage muttered, the lower half of their face visible beneath the hem of their hood curling in a grin. "In this dimension, none can defeat me."

"...Eh...?"

Mushiki swallowed his words.

He recognized that voice.

But it was impossible—inconceivable. He stared back at the figure, his eyebrows raised in shock.

The mage's shoulders trembled slightly, as though amused by his reaction—then without warning, they lowered the hood shrouding their face.

It revealed a plume of long radiant hair, glistening in the light shining from their four-layered crest.

"..."

As he took in the now-exposed figure, this time Mushiki was brought to a complete halt.

That was only natural. After all, the face staring back at him was that of—

"Saika...?"

Standing before him was Saika Kuozaki, the same figure as Mushiki himself.

"Greetings, *Me*. It's been a while... Ha. Truly an odd thing to say. I never imagined you might pull through after how I left you. But I suppose I *do* have a strong hold on life." In a relaxed tone, the mage—Saika—waved her outstretched hand.

"What...?"

Mushiki couldn't believe what he was witnessing and reached out unconsciously to touch his face, to confirm that he was still who he thought he was.

"But...*how*...?"

"Ha-ha-ha. Why are you so surprised? Hmm... Here comes your dear *Saika*—is that it? As unbelievable as this may be, don't you think you're acting a little too aloof there...? Ah, perhaps..." Saika's eyes narrowed in mirth as she looked Mushiki over. "Perhaps *you* are not, in fact, *me*?"

"...!" Mushiki was caught off guard, recoiling in surprise.

Saika let out a low chuckle. "Looks like I hit the nail on the head. I *thought* there was something odd about your reactions...but it all makes sense now. I suppose you managed to survive by merging your own life force with someone else's using a coalescence technique? Well, well, well, aren't we a dirty little creature. You would have done better to breathe your last back then," Saika said with a shrug.

Strictly speaking, Mushiki and the newly appeared Saika weren't entirely identical.

Not only were their clothes different, the other Saika's hair was tied back loosely, and the crest circling above her head had a slightly thorny shape. There were faint dark circles around her iridescent eyes, tinged, it seemed, with haggard exhaustion.

Even subtracting all those factors, it was clear from her appearance, from her bearing, that she was unmistakably Saika Kuozaki.

"Are you...really Saika...?"

"Ah. I am. And you are...?"

"...Mushiki Kuga."

"Mushiki. I see you've met with a stroke of misfortune. On behalf of *my other self*, I apologize. It looks like little old me has caused you a fair amount of trouble."

"...What do you mean? Does Saika have a twin or something? Or are you using some kind of magical technique to imitate her...?"

"Ha-ha-ha. You *do* have a vivid imagination. It's quite true that it wouldn't be impossible to copy someone's features with the right techniques, down to the smallest detail. But it would take a god to reproduce my fourth substantiation." She laughed, pointing to her chest with an outstretched thumb. "I am without a doubt Saika Kuozaki... Just from a little further along in time than you are now."

"What...?" Mushiki stood aghast at her outlandish claim. "Further along...in time...? Like, from the future...?"

Her off-the-cuff confession made no sense.

The situation was beyond imaginable, leaving him unable to process his thoughts.

However, he quickly snapped back to attention.

Kuroe's words the very first day he had arrived at the Garden resounded in his ears. *"There is the fruit of wisdom with the power to create star- or planet-destroying weapons, psychic anomalies that bring about endless natural cataclysms, swarms of golden locusts that devour everything in their path, deadly pandemics with massive fatality rates, emissaries from the future hoping to change the course of history, and a gigantic conflagration that would encompass the entire planet with its mere existence... These entities, each of them with the power to destroy the earth as we know it, we call annihilation factors."*

Right. He had heard about this sort of thing before.

How people from the future might appear hoping to change the past.

That being the case, this was an annihilation factor...

But there was a difference—in precisely who that emissary from the future was.

When you break it down, it was a remarkably simple explanation.

It would take the most powerful mage in the world to kill Saika Kuozaki, the most powerful in the world.

Even so, there were still several points that remained unclear.

"...Why would a future Saika want to kill the current one?" he asked with a grim look.

Indeed. Assuming that what she said was true, it was utterly incomprehensible that she would travel back in time with the intention of killing herself.

Future Saika gave him a brief nod before answering. "I have only one objective, and it hasn't changed for eons—to save the world and the people who call it home."

"...What do you mean?" Mushiki asked, his brow furrowed.

Future Saika stared down at the ground before continuing. "Soon, not too long from now, *my* world met with its destruction."

"...?!" Mushiki's heart skipped a beat at this shocking declaration.

Future Saika, however, ignored him as she proceeded with her story. "I, as the World King, must do everything in my power to avert it. I have to make it as though it never happened. The only way to achieve that was to take the place of my past self with my supervisory authority over the world—and to take the necessary countermeasures before the seeds of destruction could sprout... Of course, it would be necessary to disrupt the laws of cause and effect to ensure that I wouldn't cease to be even if my past self perished."

"World King...? Supervisory authority over the world...?" Mushiki repeated, further thrown off by the unfamiliar terms.

"I see that you haven't acquired my memories." Future Saika gave him a nonplussed shrug. "That's unfortunate... Or should I say, a stroke of good fortune, perhaps? There's so much information in that mind of mine that you're better off not knowing," she said, sticking her index finger to the side of her skull self-deprecatingly.

Mushiki's face contorted in confusion. "Hold on a minute. The world...is going to be destroyed? How can you say that so easily?"

"The world isn't as stable as you might think. To begin with...the real world was *already* destroyed long ago."

"...Huh...?" Unable to comprehend what Future Saika was saying, Mushiki's eyes all but spun around in circles. "What are you saying...? Then, where are we now?" he asked as he dug his foot into the ground.

Future Saika shrugged, her cheeks dimpling as she responded. "Here? The area produced by my substantiation technique, no?" She spread her hands wide as though asking him to take in the urban labyrinth that stretched out around them.

"This is no time for jokes. I meant—"

"I know what you meant. And I'm not joking. That was a genuine answer."

"Huh...?" Mushiki stared back, his mind flooding with yet more questions.

Future Saika's gaze was downcast. "Four substantiations. The first, *phenomena*; the second, *matter*; the third, *assimilation*; and the fourth, *domain*. Those are the four ranks that substantiation techniques are divided into. You're following me this far, I hope?" she asked with an exaggerated gesture.

"..." Mushiki continued to watch her in silence.

Future Saika, however, seemingly having read his thoughts, nodded. "But what lies next? Fourth substantiations are touted as supreme domains, but if a power could exist beyond them, what form would it take?"

"That's..." Mushiki stopped to consider her question.

With one's second substantiation, they created matter. With their third, they shrouded it around their body. Then with their fourth, they manifested a new domain centered around their own existence. Depending on the power of the mage responsible, such domains could encompass tremendously vast areas.

Though, to imagine something else beyond even those abilities...

"It can't be," he said.

"That's right." Future Saika's lips twisted in a smile. "One's fifth substantiation, *world*. This planet that you call Earth is nothing more than a substantiation forged by a lone mage when the real Earth was destroyed."

"..."

This revelation was so far beyond the realm of belief that it left Mushiki utterly speechless.

"Around five hundred years ago, the planet known as Earth ceased to be. At the time, I created a new identical world within my fifth substantiation and evacuated the survivors... But I wasn't able to save everyone... I told you, didn't I? This world is much more fragile than you could possibly imagine."

"..."

She puckered her lips in response to his silence. "Hmph. No response. I take it you still don't believe me?"

"Huh? Oh. No." Mushiki shook his head. "I'm not surprised to hear Saika would do something like that. I mean, that's who she is. If anything, I was just thinking how I've lived seventeen years of my life in a world she created. The air tastes beautiful here."

Future Saika's eyes rounded in surprise as she burst out laughing. "Ha-ha-ha. What are you saying? My other self chose an odd partner, I see."

Watching her carefully, Mushiki cleared his throat as if to catch his breath.

It wasn't that he understood everything she had just said. In fact, it would be no exaggeration to say that there were a great many points he still didn't fully grasp. However, he did recognize that the person across from him had somehow come back from the future to prevent the destruction of this world that he called home.

All the same, there were still several things that remained unclear. "But why do you want to kill our Saika?" he asked, staring deep into her eyes. "If you want to fix your mistakes, you could have avoided that future by advising your past self. You didn't have to—"

"That wouldn't work," Future Saika interrupted him, her voice tinged with resignation. "My past self would never have accepted my plan as it is now. My proposal may be able to save the world from destruction, but it isn't without considerable sacrifice."

"Sacrifice...?"

"That's right. At the very least, the lives of more than thirty percent of the people presently residing in my world will be required to build the foundations of a future in which it survives."

Mushiki's words stuck in his throat. "You...you would kill Saika, harm Ruri and Kuroe, and even sacrifice hundreds of millions of innocent people?"

"I, too, cannot do this without a sense of anguish. But if I don't, my entire world will be destroyed, *all* life wiped out... If I have to choose—"

"No," Mushiki interrupted her before she could finish.

"...Hah?"

"Saika would never say anything like that."

Future Saika was visibly taken aback by Mushiki's strong declaration. "Do you realize what you're saying?"

"Saika would never make a choice like that. She would find a way to save everyone, no matter the level of despair she was confronted with."

Future Saika's face contorted with indignation. "Do you think I haven't? I've tried *everything*, tested every possible avenue. This is our only hope..."

"Still, Saika would never do that. She loves this world more than anyone else."

"..." Future Saika's expression changed at once to astonishment, transcending discomfort—raw, unmistakable anger. "I didn't say it was easy... What do *you* understand?"

"I wasn't suggesting it was easy. It's just...you didn't sound like Saika just now. That's all."

Mushiki was fully aware that he was spouting nonsense.

After all, the person standing in front of him clearly was Saika Kuozaki, albeit from the future.

On top of that, he had only just merged with her and had yet to even get a good grasp of her personality and character.

Everything he knew about her was gleaned from images and recordings he saw. He had only spoken to her for the briefest of moments before his death.

To be perfectly blunt, the Saika whom he had fallen in love with at first sight might be nothing more than his own imagining, an abstract ideal. Above all, it was dangerous in the extreme to proclaim all this in front of the person herself.

Yet he felt no hesitation—only an intense conviction in his heart.

There was no way that someone so strong and powerful, someone who had altered the very course of his life, would make such a choice.

"Huh... Another *odd* outburst. If not me, then who is the true Saika Kuozaki?"

Love was blind.

Love was fanatical.

Mushiki raised his hand in front him, stretched out his thumb, and pointed to his own chest. "Right now, in this reality—me," he declared. "*I am Saika Kuozaki.*"

"Hah...? Ha-ha-ha-ha-ha-ha-ha-ha-ha!" Unable to contain herself, the future Saika burst into laughter. "What *are* you saying...? But I suppose they do say that fools shine brightest."

After raising her hands to her face as she let out another chuckle, she shot him a sharp look through her interlaced fingers. "But you seem to have misunderstood. I don't need to answer your questions. I don't need your approval or permission. My goal now is to usurp the title of World King from *you*, the me of this time and place. In other words, the only road ahead of you now is death...!"

With that, Future Saika spread her hands wide—and the crests of her second and third substantiations, already hovering above her head, radiated brilliant light.

"—!"

Mushiki squinted as he watched the light spread to her hands and body as it slowly enveloped her.

Before long, those rays of light contracted into two distinct objects—a huge mage's staff with an orb at its tip and a dress of scintillating luminescence.

Along with the crests floating above her head, these new additions truly transformed her into the very image of a witch.

The second and third substantiations of the Witch of Resplendent Color, Saika Kuozaki.

For a moment, her beauty and magnificence all but blinded Mushiki.

Even so, there was no time to spare.

"Hmm." Future Saika raised her staff, taller than she was, and then struck the ground with its tip.

In an instant, the urban labyrinth stretching out around them suddenly morphed.

"What...?!"

In its place was a raging, stormy sea.

No, not just a sea. The water's surface swelled, rising into the shape of a monster imbued with a will of its own, ensnaring Mushiki with its hands as it dragged him under.

Mushiki was snatched up by the water, caught in a whirlpool like a helpless piece of flotsam. Unable to so much as breathe, pulled under by a tremendous force latching on to his hands, legs, and torso, he felt as if his entire body was about to be twisted and ripped apart.

"...!"

Almost losing consciousness, he managed to focus his mind just long enough to leap out from the water's surface, using light-based orbs he had fashioned from his first substantiation as footholds.

"Hah... Hah..."

"Oh-ho-ho. What an impressive display of dexterity." Floating above him, Future Saika let out an amused laugh as she lifted her staff toward the heavens. "But can't you see this is the end? My fourth substantiation can paint every possible scene that might exist in this world. I will show you why people call me the Witch of Resplendent Color!"

No sooner did she finish speaking than a brilliant light radiated from her staff, and the raging ocean stretching out around her changed once again.

Plumes of smoke rose into the sky above fields of roiling lava.

In the blink of an eye, the area around Mushiki had been transformed into the mouth of an enormous volcano.

"Ngh...?!"

The scorching air nipped at his skin and nose, making it hard for him to even keep his eyes open.

Through the narrowed field of vision of his squinting eyes, he caught sight of a wave of lava—and within it, flames like a rearing dragon.

"What...?" His breath stuck in his throat.

The dragon swelled as if to show off its immense size, its huge jaw widening as it approached to consume him whole.

The word *death* flashed through his mind. The approaching dragon was a monster of pure fire. Not only would it tear through him, it would burn him to ash with a single touch.

"—"

Despite being faced with this desperate situation, Mushiki was dominated by something other than thoughts of pain and death.

At this rate, within a few seconds, his—or rather, Saika's—beautiful skin would be reduced to blackened ash.

The body of the most beautiful woman in the world.

Saika Kuozaki, whose supreme figure was beloved by the gods.

Mushiki would never tolerate such a thing.

"I won't...let you harm Saika anymore...!" he cried, raising his right hand toward the oncoming dragon.

There was no basis for his certainty, yet he was resolute.

His body, like the enemy whom he was now facing, was that of the most powerful mage ever to live, Saika Kuozaki.

There was no way that she—that this body—wouldn't know what to do.

"Aaarrrggghhh!"

The dragon engulfed him, tremendous heat in the air.

Except—

"...Oh?" Future Saika breathed in astonishment.

It was little wonder. After all, Mushiki, who by all rights should have just been swallowed by the dragon, was still there, floating before her.

"You're good, pulling out a new miracle at the last second." Future Saika's eyes narrowed in amusement as she glared at him.

"..." Faced with the intensity of that blinding light, Mushiki caught his breath, his shoulders heaving up and down.

Just a short moment ago, his throat and lungs had been exposed to so much burning air that it had hurt to breathe, but now he couldn't feel the intense heat around him.

That was as it should be. Above his head, his own three-layered crest was now bursting with light, a staff appearing in his own hand as a dazzling dress took form around him.

Yes, Saika Kuozaki's second and third substantiations.

Mushiki was now a mirror image of the Saika from the future floating before him.

"...An interesting application. I might build on it myself. Aren't you showing your hand a little too much, though?" Mushiki said, imitating Saika's tone of voice.

Her lips curled in a smile. "Interesting. But can a fake possibly keep up with the real thing?"

"*Keep up*, you say? What a strange expression. You talk like you're winning here."

"Heh..." Future Saika's smile twisted in amusement as she raised her staff into the air once more.

Mushiki, likewise, imitated her movements.

Above his head, the crest of his fourth substantiation began to unfold.

"The creation of all things."

"Heaven and earth alike reside in the palm of my hand."

"Pledge obedience."

"For I—"

"—will make of you my bride."

The moment their voices overlapped, the space surrounding them both shifted once more.

An endless horizon. A vast desert.

An eerie confluence of two separate fourth substantiations.

"Rage—"

"Ugh...!"

As though responding to both sets of commands, the wind began to roil, tearing through the sand as it wove two gigantic tornadoes.

Those sand-filled whirlpools flailed like two violent snakes, intertwining between the two figures, raging wildly, scattering them with endless sand and dirt.

"Heh, so you're not just a bigmouth! I'm impressed! I wouldn't have thought you would be able to master my techniques so well in such a short span of time! You'll have to tell me how you did it!" Future Saika burst out laughing as she twirled her staff in a circle. "But all the same... Did you really think you would be able to defeat me alone?"

As though responding to her words, the area around them shifted again, no doubt about to manifest into yet another domain.

"..."

Mushiki concentrated, paying special attention to Future Saika's every move and the flow of her magical energy.

An eerie sensation washed over him. Robed now in the dress of his third substantiation, he was able to read, somehow, the composition of the domain his opponent had begun to fashion.

"Fourth substantiation..."

Only half aware of what he was doing, Mushiki spun his own staff in a mirror image of Future Saika's movements.

Centering first around his foe, then him, the scenery was overwritten...pulling away to reveal an urban labyrinth comprised of innumerable towering structures.

Yes. Saika's next domain was none other than the very first he had witnessed.

"Yes. This is the most familiar choice. You could even call it the

landscape of my heart." Future Saika nodded with satisfaction as she showed Mushiki a soft grin. "I would love to play with you a little longer, but I'm afraid I don't have much time myself. Let's settle this."

With that, she leaped into action, flying into the sky as if gravity had somehow reversed.

"...! Wait!"

He had no idea what she was trying to achieve, but he knew that inaction would be disastrous and so, likewise, flew up into the air to meet her.

He slid up by the side of one of the towering structures surrounding them, its end far out of sight, continuing higher and higher.

Finally, Mushiki broke through the thick layer of clouds and reached the vastness of the deep-blue sky.

"This..."

As he looked out at the scene before him, his eyes widened in realization.

Towering mountains like razor-sharp swords stretched out before him.

In the distance above—the same scene, turned upside down, expanded in all directions.

He remembered this sight—he had seen it once before, after merging with Saika. It was the fourth substantiation he had used against Anviet.

Amid that landscape like the fangs of a huge beast closing in, Future Saika danced calmly through the sky as she turned her staff toward him.

"...It's over."

In response to those words, the two metropolises, above and below, began to close in to crush him.

"Ngh...!"

Mushiki in turn raised his own staff, channeled his magical energy, and commanded the world.

...But this place, half of which was supposed to have been generated by his own fourth substantiation, failed to react in any discernible way.

Future Saika gave a victorious smirk. "I told you, *Mushiki*. It's over."

She emphasized his name as she spoke, as though claiming that of Saika Kuozaki exclusively for herself.

"You've imitated me well. Whatever your reasons, your talent is commendable... But looked at from another perspective, that's all it is. To think that an imitation could ever defeat the real thing."

"Ugh..."

As Future Saika's beautiful voice penetrated his ears, his whole consciousness was submerged in darkness.

"...Huh?"

When he came to, Mushiki was sitting at a desk in what looked like a classroom.

It wasn't his room in the central school building at the Garden, but instead, it looked like a normal classroom at an ordinary school.

But was *ordinary* really the right word? There was nothing outside the window, just a pure-white void. As though this classroom existed in a dimension entirely by itself.

"This place... No, more importantly..."

A moment later, he remembered what had happened just before losing consciousness and glanced down at his hands.

"Right, Future Saika killed me...," he murmured before falling silent.

The reason was simple—those weren't Saika's hands, but his own.

It wasn't just his hands that had reverted in form. His entire body, so far as he could feel with his fingertips, had changed back to its original form. Had something prompted another state conversion?

No, maybe this was supposed to be a world beyond death? If he had breathed his last, it stood to reason that he would have regained his own body.

"Am I...dead...?" he uttered.

Strangely, he felt neither sorrow nor regret. It was like he was listening to his own voice with the composure of someone else.

"...Ugh."

Then another possibility took hold in the back of his mind, his heart tightening in alarm.

If *he* had died, that also meant Saika's body had died—and that Future Saika had chosen the worst possible outcome.

"I... I..."

He clenched his fists and slammed them down on his desk, ruing his inability to do anything about it all.

When—

"It isn't time yet for mourning. There is still more for you to do."

"...!"

A voice resounded through the air, and Mushiki looked up with a start.

His heart skipped a beat—not because of the sudden sound of the voice calling out to him nor even because of what exactly it had said.

Rather, what had startled him was that it had sounded so familiar.

"Um..."

Taken by surprise, he cast his gaze to the front of the room.

Before him was the blackboard, the teacher's lectern, and a table—and atop that table sat a girl, cool and unfazed.

"You..." He stared at her face, his words failing him.

"Even I couldn't beat her. No one in this world as it is now can. And yet..." She rose slowly to her feet. "I'll say it again. I'm glad it was you who found me."

"..."

Saika Kuozaki from the future let out a shallow breath, then deactivated her fourth substantiation.

Just as the fourth component of her crest faded away above her head, the fangs of the city that had just engulfed Mushiki dissipated, the nighttime scenery of the forecourt in the Garden reappearing in their place.

The other three layers of her crest remained activated. There may have been a clear difference between her overall strength and that of her opponent, but she was, after all, facing her former self. Until she could confirm her death, she couldn't afford to let down her guard.

Still, that was ultimately just a precaution.

She had felt a solid response upon making impact. There could be little doubt that her past self, and Mushiki Kuga along with her, had perished.

Left alone, the realm created by the former World King would begin to collapse. She had to take her former self's place before that could happen.

"...So he *was* all talk after all," she murmured with a touch of disappointment.

She didn't waste a second before rescinding that thought. Disappointment was an emotion that arose from having *expectations*. It was hardly appropriate for her to use such an expression now.

Nonetheless, she would have been lying if she had said that no pain pricked her heart. Mushiki had also been a part of Saika's beloved world. He was one of the people whom she had hoped to save.

The same was true for Ruri. She adored Saika and had always been by her side back then—so while she had no choice but to eliminate her, she had kept the damage to a level that could be addressed with adequate medical treatment. If she hadn't gone that far, Ruri would no doubt have fought to the end.

...It was all meaningless now. With a sneer of self-derision, Future Saika shook her head.

"...Now, then..."

At that moment, as she glanced around for the corpse of her past self, which should now have been freed from her fourth substantiation...

"..."

In the forecourt in front of the mansion, a solitary figure appeared, a gust of wind coursing around it.

For a moment, she thought she had seen her past self—but she was wrong.

Standing there before her was a young man, his powerless face turned downward.

His hair was light in color, his arms and legs too thin to describe as muscular. There were no distinguishing features about his silhouette.

"What...?"

As she took in his figure, her brow furrowed.

Naturally, the only individuals here were her, her past self, and the attendant who had passed out at the edge of the Garden.

"...No, it can't be..."

The moment she realized the possibility, she watched him on high alert.

"A state conversion. So the *death* of the outside body caused the original hidden form to manifest?"

"..."

Had the boy—Mushiki—reacted to those words, or was it just coincidence? In any event, he was now staring back at her.

His eyes were somewhat vacant as they scanned her face, causing her to wonder whether he was truly aware.

Future Saika, however, remained nonplussed, focusing her strength into the staff in her hand.

Yes. If Mushiki was still alive, that meant her past self wasn't entirely dead, either. She could perhaps have been in a state of suspended animation from the damage she had sustained, but so long as Mushiki, with whom her life force was intertwined, remained breathing, she would slowly heal behind the scenes.

"I'm sorry. I bear you no enmity, but I can't allow my past self to live." So saying, she raised her staff into the air once more—the crest of her fourth substantiation unfolding above her head. "I'll offer you a tribute—by giving you the same death as my past self."

All at once, the world changed form with Future Saika at its center.

A cerulean sky unfurled, towering fang-like pinnacles appearing above and below.

Among the endless landscapes made possible by her fourth substantiation, this was the closest to her original home—the distorted modern cityscape.

However, this ability, this realm, was ultimately just a by-product—the true essence of her magic lay in measuring possibilities and selecting them.

The power to manipulate fate and draw forth a desired future.

In this domain, she had no peers.

"Fourth Substantiation: Void's Garden."

As she spoke, a cluster of towering structures closed in on Mushiki like the jaw of a mighty beast.

He didn't move. Or was it more correct to say he *couldn't* move? He simply stood there in quiet acceptance of the oncoming death.

Soon, fangs touched fangs, overlapping each other as they fell to crush Mushiki between them.

Only—

"...Huh?"

The next moment, Future Saika's eyebrows quivered in surprise.

Those twin rows of monoliths were entwined together—when a small crack ruptured through the middle, that solid outer wall collapsing like a sandcastle.

"What...?"

She had never before witnessed such a phenomenon and, for a long moment, doubted her own eyes.

Then, from amid that collapsing rubble...

"..."

...Mushiki emerged without a scratch.

"No..." Words failed Future Saika as she watched from a distance.

This was to be expected.

After all, above Mushiki's head now hovered a transparent crest forged from what could have been horns or barbs.

"..."

Thinner, thinner again.

He felt like his essence was being honed, polished.

Broader, much broader.

A sense as of melting into the wider world.

Mushiki, having reverted from Saika's form back to his own, was staring straight ahead at Future Saika through the crumbling debris.

It was a strange feeling.

An eerie sense of omnipotence, just as when he had first wielded magic in the guise of Saika's body.

However, now he was himself. There was no way he could be wielding Saika's magic here.

Yes, the only abilities available to him as he was now...

...were his own.

"Ah..."

Of course, he had never used these powers before, not even once.

What form did they take? What were their abilities? How was he supposed to train them, develop them? He didn't have the faintest clue.

But even so.

Yes, even so.

Mushiki, a novice mage, had accumulated experiences that by all means should have been impossible.

Now feelings that should not have existed did.

The strongest mage. Saika Kuozaki.

These hands now knew what it felt like to have wielded the powers of the World King, the pride of Saika Kuozaki.

All that remained was to carefully re-create them.

If he could do that...

If he could do that, Mushiki Kuga's own innate magic, powers that shouldn't have existed anywhere in the world, would come to life.

"So you're a mage, too? That's an odd technique you're weaving," Future Saika, floating in the air before him, said with narrowed eyes. "But so what? What can you possibly hope to achieve with a fragile first substantiation like that?"

That was exactly what Mushiki himself wanted to know. His own new techniques had just come into being. Not even he had a clear grasp on them.

Yet be that as it may, he had already decided on his response to Future Saika's jeer. "I'll save you."

"...Tch." Future Saika looked furious at this direct remark. "Did I mishear you just now? *You* mean to save *me*?"

She stared down at him, her eyes burning with contempt, indignation, and agitation.

Mushiki slowly looked up. "Saika, your goal isn't to take the place of your present-day self but to save the world from destruction... Right?"

"...What of it?"

Mushiki pointed to his chest with his thumb. "If we can prevent that future, that would mean you don't have to kill our Saika."

"Enough with these games. How can *you* possibly overturn a wave of destruction that *I* couldn't even escape?!"

"...Yeah, I know it won't be easy. But at the very least...there's one crucial difference between you and the present-day Saika."

"...And what would that be?"

Mushiki stared straight into her eyes as he answered her. "Me. I'll save you... It's thanks to you that I got to meet my Saika... It's thanks to you that my destiny was changed... So I'll never let you choose a course of action that will ruin you like this...!"

"...!"

Future Saika's breath caught in her throat for a moment—but her countenance soon twisted in anger. "Don't get carried away. You're just an ordinary person who happened to stumble on my deathbed... You know nothing of the end of the world, of the heavens cracking and the earth splitting open... You know nothing of despair, of the screams of countless innocents... You haven't watched as your world and everyone you love dies before your very eyes...!"

Then, looking as if she might burst into tears, she screamed. "I won't say that what I'm doing is *right*. I don't care if you denounce me as a villain. But I...I *will* kill you to save this world...!" she cried, giving him a murderous glare.

Mushiki met her gaze head-on. "In that case, to save you, I will defeat you."

"What utter nonsense...!" Future Saika shouted—and as her voice echoed, fresh spires manifested behind her.

All at once, their tips turned toward Mushiki and unleashed a tremendous blast of magical energy.

Each one of those barrages was a lethal blow, brilliant bursts of light in every color imaginable.

They coursed toward him, too many to possibly count.

Yet Mushiki, even faced with this desperate situation, was filled with a strange sense of calm.

"I couldn't use my Saika's magic to beat you. That's only natural. After all, you're the real thing. But," he said, still staring at her through the blinding light, "there's one part of me that could never lose to you."

As his vision flooded with rainbow-colored light, his thoughts grew sharper, more finely honed.

If he died here, Future Saika would, as she had already declared, take whatever measures she thought necessary to save the world.

Even knowing that so many lives would be lost by her doing so.

To save a greater number, she would discard those whom she loved more than anything else.

Mushiki couldn't allow her to do that.

"Second Substantiation..."

From deep in the emptiness of his consciousness, a soft voice emitted—and above his head, his crest unfolded with a second layer.

"...Hollow Edge."

As though answering his call, magical energy converged around his arm to forge a sword, a transparent blade like glass.

A fleeting weapon, so ephemeral that light itself might break it.

"The one thing that you will never defeat..." Mushiki spoke with deep conviction as he brought the only thing capable of stopping the strongest witch in the world swooping down. "...is my love for Saika!"

He directed the tip of his narrow blade her way—toward the oncoming, raging, murderous force coursing toward him.

"Descend, my illusion...!" Future Saika cried out, wielding the staff of her second substantiation.

Answering her call, a plume of magic-infused light, too enormous to simply call a ray, slammed hard into Mushiki.

It was a devastating attack, the Witch of Resplendent Color's magic all focused into one shot. If it had hit any ordinary person, it wouldn't have left so much as bone remaining.

Indeed, if not for his fourth substantiation, the deadly blow would have ended not only his own life but would have devastated the surrounding landscape far into the distance.

And yet—

"...?!"

The next moment, Future Saika recoiled in alarm.

The light filling her field of vision split open—and Mushiki was closing in on her.

"Impossible..."

In his right hand, he held a transparent sword, and above his head hovered two new crests, rippling like the surface of a lake.

Both of those crests seemed to be comprised of horn- or thorn-like pieces.

As the two overlapped, the impression they gave was that of a royal crown.

"..."

There was no sound, and nothing vocalized.

Mushiki's sword plunged deep into her chest.

A magical barrier shielded her body, as did the dress created by her third substantiation.

Yet the blade passed through both without any resistance.

"Ah..." A faint gasp escaped her lips.

There was no pain. Not even a drop of blood flowed down her chest.

Instead, the staff in her hand, the dress covering her body, and the crests radiating above her head shattered like broken pieces of glasswork.

In a haze of sparkling light, her substantiations faded into the air around her.

"..."

Taking in this fantastic scene, she was struck by a mysterious sensation.

It wasn't quite humiliation, nor regret, nor despair at having failed to save the world.

It was the essence of her magic, the power to manipulate fate and draw forth a desired future.

So long as her fourth substantiation had been activated, none could escape its intrinsic laws.

That being the case, was this outcome the end result...?

"...Ha." She gave a weak laugh.

"..."

Below a sky dyed a myriad of colors, Mushiki, having wielded his blade half in a daze, somehow managed to calm his breathing and keep his consciousness from flickering out.

He couldn't afford to slip into darkness here, not now. Or to let his life force slip away.

This was the first time he had ever used his own innate magic, and his body had let out a tremendous wail of anguish in response. But through that, he had managed to keep his eyes open by focusing on one thing—his feelings for Saika.

So it wasn't until he felt something soft stroking his head that he realized where he was.

"Huh...?"

Saika was patting his head.

His mind finally processing the present scene, he looked up.

Before him was Saika in the flesh, surrounded by light and smiling fondly at him.

"So you aren't just a bigmouth. You won't let the other me choose the same path I did, will you?"

As she spoke, cracks began to emanate through the sky around her, spreading out in all directions as the space surrounding them crumbled.

"Saika..." Mushiki tried calling out her name, but his voice failed him.

His awareness, having long passed its limits, was already sinking into the darkness.

The only sound to reach his ears was Saika's voice. "Look after the other me, Mushiki."

Chapter 6
⇌ Proposal ⇌

When Mushiki next regained consciousness, he found himself looking out at the same scene as when he had first arrived at the Garden.

"Ah..."

A large bedroom. A huge canopy bed. Antique furniture. Thick carpets. Everything, even down to the angle of the morning sun cutting across the room, was like a reenactment of his first time here.

There could be no doubt about it. He was in Saika's bedroom in her mansion. For a moment, he wondered whether he hadn't slipped back in time.

No. As he sat up in bed, he noticed one crucial difference.

Right now, he was in his own body, not Saika's.

His mind cleared, and his hazy memories came together to form a picture.

The situation that he had found himself in. Fighting against a Saika from the future. And then...

"...Future Saika..."

Just as he was about to climb down from the bed in his haste—

"Oh, so you're awake?" came a voice from his side.

"Ah..." Taken by surprise, he glanced across the room.

There, sitting alone in a chair, was Kuroe.

"...!"

Mushiki's eyes widened in astonishment as he all but fell from the bed, hitting his head on the floor with a tremendous thud.

"Owww..."

"There's no need to panic. I'm not going to run away," Kuroe said with a shrug.

"..."

In silence, Mushiki lifted himself up from the floor and knelt down on one knee.

...Yes, much like a knight in the service of a royal princess.

"What happened? You look different. Did you have a change of heart?" Kuroe asked, tilting her head inquisitively.

"Thank you, Saika," Mushiki said as he looked up at her.

"...Huh?" Kuroe answered, raising one eyebrow in consternation.

He lacked definitive proof, but in his heart, he was certain.

"You say some strange things," Kuroe said. "What makes you think I'm Saika?"

"It's difficult to put it into words...but if I had to say...your aura, maybe?"

"Oh...? Ha—ha-ha-ha." Kuroe, apparently finding his response amusing, broke into laughter. "I see, I see... So you saw through me so easily. Perhaps I should have expected no less of you, Mushiki."

Then, after a brief chuckle, she gave him a kind smile. "It feels like it's been a long time since I was last in a situation like this... But yes, I am Saika Kuozaki, headmistress of Void's Garden. You've done well, Mushiki."

"Thank you."

This honor, an acknowledgment from Saika herself, was more than he deserved. Mushiki bowed his head in gratitude.

Then, quickly remembering something, he looked up. "Ah, right! Are you okay? Your injuries?"

"Don't worry. That body is being repaired as we speak," Kuroe—or rather, Saika—responded with a wave of her hand.

Her explanation struck Mushiki as somewhat puzzling.

"*That body...?*"

"Ah. Strictly speaking, the body you saw yesterday and this one now are different. Both are experimental homunculi. Their composition is very close to that of regular human beings, but they have no souls. They're essentially living dolls. I prepared them to serve as refuges for my soul—substitute bodies, you could say—in the event that something should happen to me. Though, I never suspected I would have to use them so soon."

"*Homunculi...?*" Mushiki repeated in a daze.

"Yes." Saika nodded. "So long as my original body is still alive, my assailant would attempt to strike again. As such, I disguised myself as Saika Kuozaki's attendant to support you... I must apologize. I did want to reveal myself sooner, but I was cautious. I didn't know the full extent of our enemy's strength."

"N-no, it's okay..." Mushiki shook his head.

...So Kuroe had been Saika all along.

Knowing that, everything that had happened since he had merged with her and had been brought to this Garden, from the first event to the last, took on new meaning.

He had been alongside her this whole time, all while occupying her original body.

"..."

"What's wrong?"

"It's like they say, true happiness really is close at hand."

"...I mean it; is something wrong?" Saika asked, cocking her head to one side with a raised eyebrow.

Perhaps realizing that that question wouldn't provide much in the way of a response, she stood up from her chair. "Mushiki," she began. "Again, I thank you. I truly am in your debt. That's no joke—without you, I would have died... I never would have imagined that my future self might travel back in time to kill me," she said with a hint of self-derision.

At these words, Mushiki lifted his face. "Right, about that. What happened to the future you? I passed out, so..."

Saika averted her gaze. "She's already gone. I suspect her life force ran out."

"...?! I couldn't have—"

Saika stopped him there with a shake of her head. "She said the world was destroyed in the future... The World King and the world itself are one and the same. She must have already been close to her limit. So it isn't your fault. Don't make the mistake of blaming yourself for her death."

After that stern remonstration, Saika's expression relaxed. "One thing is certain—the fact that you are still alive is proof that you won... So stand proud. You surpassed me—albeit under special circumstances."

"...! No, I could never surpass you. I just kind of lost myself, and then one thing led to another..."

"Ha-ha. So I lost to someone who didn't even have full control over his magic? Maybe I ought to give *you* the title of strongest mage?" Saika joked.

Mushiki shrugged in gratitude and embarrassment.

Then, flashing him another smile, Saika added, "Now, then. You're the one who saved this world, and you deserve to be properly rewarded. Under normal circumstances, I would like to see you properly compensated and offer to let you return to the outside..." She paused for a moment before continuing: "But unfortunately, it won't be that easy. My body is still merged with yours. And above all, my future self left behind a terrible legacy—her prophecy that in the not-too-distant future, the world *will* be destroyed. She provided us with no more information to go on... So I'm sorry to have to say this, but I don't think I'll be able to let you go free. At least not until we find a way to separate my body from yours." She spoke with authority, though her face was apologetic.

Mushiki shook his head. "I made a promise with the future Saika. I'll find a way to save the world. You'll just make me angry if you try to stop me."

"Mushiki..." Saika seemed somewhat surprised for a moment but quickly looked away as she shook her head. "Ah... Yes, I see. You *are* that kind of person... You really should value your own life a little more."

Despite her words, she seemed slightly amused. Then, staring into his eyes, she said, "In that case, Mushiki, I command you."

"Yes."

"Become the other half of my body and keep on saving the world until the time comes for us to separate."

"Er, I don't like the sound of that."

"..." Saika stared back at him in all seriousness. "Can't you just go along with it for now?"

"I don't like the second part. About having to separate at some later date," Mushiki said.

"...Oh?" Saika answered, her eyebrows climbing up her forehead. "I see. If you're so determined, I suppose it would be an insult to ask you to reconsider." Still staring into his eyes, she extended her hand. "Then dedicate yourself to me. Save the world by my side."

"With pleasure," Mushiki answered without hesitation as he took her hand in his own. "Also, once this crisis is over, and if we find a way to separate our bodies, I do have one request."

"Oh? Then ask," Saika said, watching him with piqued interest.

Mushiki looked straight back into her eyes as he answered: "Give me the right to propose to you."

"...What did you just say?" Saika muttered, her eyes widening in surprise.

After a brief second, she showed him a soft smile. "Very well. I look forward to it."

⊰ Afterword ⊱

Greetings. Or if we're meeting again, it's an absolute pleasure. Koushi Tachibana here.

Thank you for reading my latest work, *King's Proposal: The Witch of Resplendent Color*. A new series is always an exciting thing, don't you think? I do hope you enjoyed it.

You might have read my previous series, *Date A Live*. So what comes next after a date? What else but a proposal! That was the train of thought that helped me arrive at this title. Maybe I'll have to call my next series *How to Greet Your In-Laws?*

I started working on this new series roughly two years ago, and from the very beginning, I've been discussing with my editor on how to include a certain unusual element in it, even if the main plot follows a common pattern.

As a result, we combined the hero and the heroine into one.

Also, as I wrote it, the protagonist ended up becoming a little bit *different*.

His sister, too, might come across as a little *strange*.

Hold on, did I say *one* unusual element?!

Now then, it's time for me to express my thanks to everyone involved in getting this new volume out there.

Continuing on from *Date A Live*, Tsunako has once again provided us with some wonderful illustrations. Saika truly is beautiful in the drawings.

Not only that, the cover was again handled by Tsuyoshi Kusano. His bold and stylish design sense shines through once more.

Of course, I have the same editor again as last time, so this really is a reunion of the team behind the last series. Well, that's the overall vibe—you could say that we haven't disbanded just yet.

I would also like to express my heartfelt thanks to all of the editorial staff; everyone involved in sales, publishing, and distribution; and of course, to you, the reader, for having picked up this book.

If you take a quick look at the cover, the number 1 is front and center, so we're definitely going to need a second volume to follow suit. I remember discussing it with my editor, a little worried that if there was no follow-up, it would just become a mysterious line running down the middle of the page...

And so with that, I look forward to seeing you again in Volume 2 of *King's Proposal*!

August 2021, Koushi Tachibana